William Shakespeare's
The Tempest
In Plain and Simple English

BookCaps™ Study Guides
www.bookcaps.com

W9-ADS-526

Table of Contents

About This Series

The "Classic Retold" series started as a way of telling classics for the modern reader—being careful to preserve the themes and integrity of the original. Whether you want to understand Shakespeare a little more or are trying to get a better grasp of the Greek classics, there is a book waiting for you!

The series is expanding every month. Visit BookCaps.com to see all the books in the series, and while you are there join the Facebook page, so you are first to know when a new book comes out.

Characters

ALONSO, King of Naples

SEBASTIAN, his Brother

PROSPERO, the right Duke of Milan

ANTONIO, his Brother, the usurping Duke of Milan

FERDINAND, Son to the King of Naples

GONZALO, an honest old counselor

ADRIAN, Lord

FRANCISCO,Lord

CALIBAN, a savage and deformed Slave

TRINCULO, a Jester

STEPHANO, a drunken Butler

MASTER OF A SHIP BOATSWAIN MARINERS

MIRANDA, Daughter to Prospero

ARIEL, an airy Spirit

IRIS, presented by Spirits

CERES, presented by Spirits

JUNO, presented by Spirits

NYMPHS, presented by Spirits

REAPERS, presented by Spirits

Other Spirits attending on Prospero

ACT I

SCENE I.
On a ship at sea: a tempestuous noise of thunder and lightning heard.
Enter a Master and a Boatswain

Master
Boatswain!
Boatswain!

Boatswain
Here, master: what cheer?
Right here, master: how goes it?

Master
Good, speak to the mariners: fall to't, yarely,
Good man, speak to the sailers: get on it, quickly,
or we run ourselves aground: bestir, bestir.
Or we will run ourselves into the shore: get busy, get busy.

Exit

Enter Mariners

Boatswain
Heigh, my hearts! cheerly, cheerly, my hearts!
Come on, comrades! With energy, with energy, comrades!
yare, yare! Take in the topsail. Tend to the
At once, at once! Take in the topsail. Listen for the
master's whistle. Blow, till thou burst thy wind,
Master's whistles. Wind you can blow all you want,
if room enough!
If there's enough room between ship and shore!

Enter ALONSO, SEBASTIAN, ANTONIO, FERDINAND, GONZALO, and others

ALONSO
Good boatswain, have care. Where's the master?
Good boatswain, take care. Where's the master?
Play the men.
Get the men to work.

Boatswain
I pray now, keep below.
Please, stay below.

ANTONIO
Where is the master, boatswain?
Where's the master, boatswain?

Boatswain
Do you not hear him? You mar our labour: keep your
Can't you hear him? You're hampering our work: stay in your
cabins: you do assist the storm.
Cabins: you're really helping the storm.

GONZALO
Nay, good, be patient.
No, good man, be patient.

Boatswain
When the sea is. Hence! What cares these roarers
I'll be patient when the sea is. Go away! What do these roaring waves care
for the name of king? To cabin: silence! trouble us not.
About the name of a king? Go into your cabin: be silent! Don't trouble us.

GONZALO
Good, yet remember whom thou hast aboard.
Good man, you must remember whom you have aboard.

Boatswain
None that I more love than myself. You are a
No one that I love more than myself. You are an
counsellor; if you can command these elements to
Advisor; if you can command the winds and water to
silence, and work the peace of the present, we will
Silence, and put this present affair to rest, we won't
not hand a rope more; use your authority: if you
Handle a rope again; use your power: if you
cannot, give thanks you have lived so long, and make
Can't, then be thankful you have lived so long, and prepare
yourself ready in your cabin for the mischance of
Yourself in your cabin incase disaster strikes
the hour, if it so hap. Cheerly, good hearts! Out

At this moment. Energetically, good comrades! Get out
of our way, I say.
Of our way, I say.

Exit

GONZALO
I have great comfort from this fellow: methinks he
I have a good feeling about this fellow: it seems to me that he
hath no drowning mark upon him; his complexion is
Doesn't look like a man who will drown; his look is of one
perfect gallows. Stand fast, good Fate, to his
Who will die of hanging instead. Good Fate, remain set on his
hanging: make the rope of his destiny our cable,
Hanging: make it so that the rope of his hanging is an anchor line,
for our own doth little advantage. If he be not
For our own line is going us very little good. If he wasn't
born to be hanged, our case is miserable.
Born to be hanged, our situation is dire.

Exeunt

Re-enter Boatswain

Boatswain
Down with the topmast! yare! lower, lower! Bring
Bring the topmast down! Now! Lower, lower! Separate
her to try with main-course.
It from the mailsail.

A cry within

A plague upon this howling! they are louder than
Curse this crying! These people are louder than
the weather or our office.
The weather or our work.

Re-enter SEBASTIAN, ANTONIO, and GONZALO

Yet again! what do you here? Shall we give o'er
Yet again! What are you doing here? Should we give in
and drown? Have you a mind to sink?
And drown? Do you want to sink?

SEBASTIAN
A pox o' your throat, you bawling, blasphemous,
Curse your yelling, you hollering, offensive,
incharitable dog!
Heartless sea-dog!

Boatswain
Work you then.
Get to work then.

ANTONIO
Hang, cur! hang, you whoreson, insolent noisemaker!
Blast you, dog! Blast you, you son of a whore, disrespectful bellower!
We are less afraid to be drowned than thou art.
We are less afraid of drowning than you are.

GONZALO
I'll warrant him for drowning; though the ship were
I'll make sure he doesn't drown; even if this ship was
no stronger than a nutshell and as leaky as an
No stronger than a nutshell, and was as wet as an
unstanched wench.
Unsatisfied whore.

Boatswain
Lay her a-hold, a-hold! set her two courses off to
Bring the ship into the wind, into the wind! Set her compass out to
sea again; lay her off.
Sea again; bring her away from land.

Enter Mariners wet

Mariners
All lost! to prayers, to prayers! all lost!
All is lost! Pray, everyone pray! All is lost!

Boatswain
What, must our mouths be cold?
What, must we die?

GONZALO
The king and prince at prayers! let's assist them,
The king and prince get to praying! Let's help them,
For our case is as theirs.

For our fate is the same as theirs.

SEBASTIAN
I'm out of patience.
I'm out of patience.

ANTONIO
We are merely cheated of our lives by drunkards:
We've just been cheated out of our lives by drunks:
This wide-chapp'd rascal--would thou mightst lie drowning
And this big-mouthed scoundrel—I wish you would lie drowning
The washing of ten tides!
And washed over by ten tides!

GONZALO
He'll be hang'd yet,
He'll still be hanged eventually,
Though every drop of water swear against it
Even though every drop of water indicates otherwise
And gape at widest to glut him.
And open up widest to take him.

A confused noise within: 'Mercy on us!'-- 'We split, we split!'--'Farewell, my wife and children!'--'Farewell, brother!'--'We split, we split, we split!'

[A confused noise within: 'Mercy on us'—'We're sinking, we're sinking!'—'Good bye, my wife and children!'—'Goodbye, brother!'—'We're sinking, we're sinking, we're sinking!']

ANTONIO
Let's all sink with the king.
Let's all sink with the kind.

SEBASTIAN
Let's take leave of him.
Let's say good bye to him.

Exeunt ANTONIO and SEBASTIAN

GONZALO
Now would I give a thousand furlongs of sea for an
Right now I would trade a hundred and twenty-five miles of sea for an
acre of barren ground, long heath, brown furze, any
Acre of dry ground, with tall heather, brown evergreen shrubs, any
thing. The wills above be done! but I would fain

Thing. The lord's wish will be done! But I would desire
die a dry death.
To die a dry death.

Exeunt

SCENE II.

The island. Before PROSPERO'S cell.

Enter PROSPERO and MIRANDA

MIRANDA
If by your art, my dearest father, you have
If with your skills, my dearest father, you have
Put the wild waters in this roar, allay them.
Made the wild waters into this storm, call it off.
The sky, it seems, would pour down stinking pitch,
The sky, it seems, would like to pour down black tar,
But that the sea, mounting to the welkin's cheek,
Except for the sea, rising up to heaven,
Dashes the fire out. O, I have suffered
Puts the fire out. Oh, I have suffered
With those that I saw suffer: a brave vessel,
Along side those that I saw suffering: a well-crafted vessel
Who had, no doubt, some noble creature in her,
Who had, no doubt, some great person on board,
Dash'd all to pieces. O, the cry did knock
Crashed into pieces. Oh, the cry hit me
Against my very heart. Poor souls, they perish'd.
To my very core. Poor souls, they died.
Had I been any god of power, I would
If I were any god of power, I would
Have sunk the sea within the earth or ere
Have buried the sea within the earth before
It should the good ship so have swallow'd and
It could have swallowed up that good ship and
The fraughting souls within her.
The people carried on board.

PROSPERO
Be collected:
Calm yourself:
No more amazement: tell your piteous heart
Don't be distracted by it: tell your upset heart
There's no harm done.
That no harm has been done.

MIRANDA
O, woe the day!
Oh, no harm you call it!

PROSPERO

No harm.
No harm.
I have done nothing but in care of thee,
I have nothing except to care for you,
Of thee, my dear one, thee, my daughter, who
For you, my dear one, you, my daughter, who
Art ignorant of what thou art, nought knowing
Don't know who you are, don't know
Of whence I am, nor that I am more better
Where I am from, or that I am much better
Than Prospero, master of a full poor cell,
Than Prospero, in control of an entire small cell,
And thy no greater father.
And a position no more powerful than simply your father.

MIRANDA

More to know
Knowing more than that
Did never meddle with my thoughts.
Never concerned my thoughts.

PROSPERO

'Tis time
it's timet that
I should inform thee farther. Lend thy hand,
I told you more. Give me your hand,
And pluck my magic garment from me. So:
And take my magic cloak from me. So:

Lays down his mantle (cloak)

Lie there, my art. Wipe thou thine eyes; have comfort.
Lie there, my magic. Wipe your eyes; and take comfort in this.
The direful spectacle of the wreck, which touch'd
The terrible scene of the wreck, which touched
The very virtue of compassion in thee,
That most compassionate heart of yours,
I have with such provision in mine art
I have with careful thinking ahead in my magic
So safely ordered that there is no soul—
Safely arranged so that there is no soul—
No, not so much perdition as an hair

No, not even the loss of an hair
Betid to any creature in the vessel
Happened to any creature aboard that ship
Which thou heard'st cry, which thou saw'st sink. Sit down;
Which you heard cry out, which you saw sink. Sit down;
For thou must now know farther.
For you must now learn more.

MIRANDA
You have often
You have often
Begun to tell me what I am, but stopp'd
Begun to tell me who I am, but stopped
And left me to a bootless inquisition,
And left me with useless questions,
Concluding 'Stay: not yet.'
Concluding 'Wait: not yet.'

PROSPERO
The hour's now come;
The hour has come;
The very minute bids thee ope thine ear;
The very minute askes you to open you ears;
Obey and be attentive. Canst thou remember
Listen and be attentive. Can you remember
A time before we came unto this cell?
A time before we came to this cell?
I do not think thou canst, for then thou wast not
I don't think you cant, for you were not
Out three years old.
Yet three years old then.

MIRANDA
Certainly, sir, I can.
Certainly, sir, I can.

PROSPERO
By what? by any other house or person?
By what means? Was it any other house or person?
Of any thing the image tell me that
Tell me about the image of any thing that
Hath kept with thy remembrance.
Has stayed in your memory.

MIRANDA

'Tis far off

It's far off

And rather like a dream than an assurance

And more like a dream than a certainty

That my remembrance warrants. Had I not

That my memory sustains. Didn't I have

Four or five women once that tended me?

Four or five women who once took care of me?

PROSPERO

Thou hadst, and more, Miranda. But how is it

You had that, and more, Miranda. But how is it

That this lives in thy mind? What seest thou else

That you remember this? What else do you see

In the dark backward and abysm of time?

In the dark past and deep chasm of time?

If thou remember'st aught ere thou camest here,

If you remember anything before you came here,

How thou camest here thou mayst.

Then you may remember how you came here.

MIRANDA

But that I do not.

But I do not remember that.

PROSPERO

Twelve year since, Miranda, twelve year since,

Twelve years ago, Miranda, twelve years ago,

Thy father was the Duke of Milan and

Your father was the Duke of Milan and

A prince of power.

A prince of power.

MIRANDA

Sir, are not you my father?

Sir, aren't you my father?

PROSPERO

Thy mother was a piece of virtue, and

Your mother was a model of virtue, and

She said thou wast my daughter; and thy father

She said you were my daughter; and your father

Was Duke of Milan; and thou his only heir

Was Duke of Milan; and you were his only heir
And princess no worse issued.
And princess of no lower position.

MIRANDA
O the heavens!
Oh, good heavens!
What foul play had we, that we came from thence?
What evil conspiracy was there against us that we came from there?
Or blessed was't we did?
Or was it a good thing that we did?

PROSPERO
Both, both, my girl:
Both, it was both, my girl:
By foul play, as thou say'st, were we heaved thence,
It was an evil conspiracy, as you said, that we were cast out of there,
But blessedly holp hither.
But fortunately helped to get here.

MIRANDA
O, my heart bleeds
Oh my heart aches
To think o' the teen that I have turn'd you to,
To think of the grief that I have brought up again,
Which is from my remembrance! Please you, farther.
From my memories! Please, continue.

PROSPERO
My brother and thy uncle, call'd Antonio—
My brother, your uncle, named Antonio--
I pray thee, mark me--that a brother should
Please. Pay attention—how could a brother
Be so perfidious!--he whom next thyself
Be so deceitful!—he, who, next to you
Of all the world I loved and to him put
Out of everyone in the world, I love and to him I gave
The manage of my state; as at that time
The task of managing of my government; since at the time
Through all the signories it was the first
Out of all the provinces it was the highest
And Prospero the prime duke, being so reputed
And I, Prospoer, the chief duke, had a reputation
In dignity, and for the liberal arts

Of honor, and for the arts and sciences
Without a parallel; those being all my study,
That was without parallel; those took up all my studying,
The government I cast upon my brother
And the governing I threw on to my brother
And to my state grew stranger, being transported
And I became a foreigner to my province, being captivated
And rapt in secret studies. Thy false uncle—
And absorbed in my magical studies. Your deceitful uncle—
Dost thou attend me?
Are you listening to me?

MIRANDA
Sir, most heedfully.
Sir, most attentively.

PROSPERO
Being once perfected how to grant suits,
Having been instructed on how to grant formal petitions,
How to deny them, who to advance and who
How to deny them, who to promote and who
To trash for over-topping, new created
To hold back for getting ahead of themselves, having newly appointed
The creatures that were mine, I say, or changed 'em,
The officials that were mine, or, I say, having replaced them,
Or else new form'd 'em; having both the key
Or else retrained them, having both the power
Of officer and office, set all hearts i' the state
Of officials and the role of office, he set all the minds in the government
To what tune pleased his ear; that now he was
To whatever message he desired; now he was
The ivy which had hid my princely trunk,
The ivy that had grown over the tree trunk of my own right to rule,
And suck'd my verdure out on't. Thou attend'st not.
And sucked my liveliness out with it. You aren't listening.

MIRANDA
O, good sir, I do.
Oh, good sir, I am.

PROSPERO
I pray thee, mark me.
Please, listen to me.
I, thus neglecting worldly ends, all dedicated

I, having neglected endeavors in this world, completely dedicated
To closeness and the bettering of my mind
To solitude and the bettering of my mind
With that which, but by being so retired,
With things which, except that they were so secluded,
O'er-prized all popular rate, in my false brother
Would be overvalued by the common consensus, in my deceitful brother
Awaked an evil nature; and my trust,
This awakened an evil nature; and my trust,
Like a good parent, did beget of him
Like a good parent, did create in him
A falsehood in its contrary as great
A disloyalty that was the complete opposite but as great
As my trust was; which had indeed no limit,
As my trust had been; which in fact had no limit,
A confidence sans bound. He being thus lorded,
A confidence without boundaries. In that was, he was made a lord,
Not only with what my revenue yielded,
Not only through what my income produced,
But what my power might else exact, like one
But also what my authority might obtain, like one
Who having into truth, by telling of it,
Who having said something against the truth, because he told it,
Made such a sinner of his memory,
Made such an impostor of his memory
To credit his own lie, he did believe
That it gave credit to his own lie, he did believe
He was indeed the duke; out o' the substitution
He was actually the duke; because he substituted in my place of authority
And executing the outward face of royalty,
And fulfilled the outward face of royalty,
With all prerogative: hence his ambition growing—
With all its privileges: from here his ambition grew—
Dost thou hear?
Do you hear what I'm saying?

MIRANDA
Your tale, sir, would cure deafness.
Your story, sir, would cure deafness.

PROSPERO
To have no screen between this part he play'd
In order to have no separation between this role he was performing
And him he play'd it for, he needs will be

And the one who he was performing it for—that is myself—he desired to become
Absolute Milan. Me, poor man, my library
The absolute ruler of Milan. For me, poor man, my library
Was dukedom large enough: of temporal royalties
Was a large enough dukedom: of wordly power
He thinks me now incapable; confederates—
He thought I was now incapable; he was allies—
So dry he was for sway--wi' the King of Naples
He was so thirty for power—with the King of Naples
To give him annual tribute, do him homage,
And had to give him annual taxes, to pay him homage,
Subject his coronet to his crown and bend
And subject his lesser crown to the greater ruler and lowered
The dukedom yet unbow'd--alas, poor Milan!—
The province that hadn't yet been overcome—sadly, poor Milan!—
To most ignoble stooping.
To a very shameful position.

MIRANDA
O the heavens!
Oh, good heavens±

PROSPERO
Mark his condition and the event; then tell me
Notice his agreement and the outcome; then tell me
If this might be a brother.
If you think a brother could do this.

MIRANDA
I should sin
It would be a sin
To think but nobly of my grandmother:
To think badly of my grandmother:
Good wombs have borne bad sons.
But good women have given birth to bad sons.

PROSPERO
Now the condition.
Now the agreement.
The King of Naples, being an enemy
The King of Naples, being an enemy
To me inveterate, hearkens my brother's suit;
Of mine for a long time, paid attention to my brothers proposition;
Which was, that he, in lieu o' the premises

Which was, that he, in place of the pledges
Of homage and I know not how much tribute,
Of homage and I'm not sure how much taxes,
Should presently extirpate me and mine
Would instead immediately eliminate me and my family
Out of the dukedom and confer fair Milan
From the province and give over the beautiul Milan
With all the honours on my brother: whereon,
With all the it's powers to my brother: After this,
A treacherous army levied, one midnight
A treacherous army was enlisted, and one midnight,
Fated to the purpose did Antonio open
Destined for this task, Antonio opened
The gates of Milan, and, i' the dead of darkness,
The gates of Milan and in the dead of night,
The ministers for the purpose hurried thence
The agents of this plan hurried to
Me and thy crying self.
Me and your crying self.

MIRANDA
Alack, for pity!
What a shame, what a pity!
I, not remembering how I cried out then,
I now, since I don't remember how I cried then,
Will cry it o'er again: it is a hint
Will cry over it again: it is a situation
That wrings mine eyes to't.
That forces my eyes to weep.

PROSPERO
Hear a little further
Listen a little more
And then I'll bring thee to the present business
And then I'll get to the current business
Which now's upon's; without the which this story
That is now upon us; without which this story
Were most impertinent.
Would be beside the point.

MIRANDA
Wherefore did they not
Why did they not
That hour destroy us?

Destroy us then?

PROSPERO
Well demanded, wench:
Good question, girl:
My tale provokes that question. Dear, they durst not,
My story invites that question. My dear, they didn't dare,
So dear the love my people bore me, nor set
So dear was the love my people had for me, nor did they dare to place
A mark so bloody on the business, but
Such a bloody mark on their business, but
With colours fairer painted their foul ends.
Painted a prettier picture of their evil plan.
In few, they hurried us aboard a bark,
In short, they hurried us aboard a ship,
Bore us some leagues to sea; where they prepared
And carried us some miles out into the sea; where they prepared
A rotten carcass of a boat, not rigg'd,
The rotting remains of a boat, without ropes,
Nor tackle, sail, nor mast; the very rats
Without gear, sail, and mast; even the rats
Instinctively had quit it: there they hoist us,
Instinctively had left it: there they left us,
To cry to the sea that roar'd to us, to sigh
To cry to the sea that roared back at us, to sigh
To the winds whose pity, sighing back again,
To the winds whose pity, sighing back again,
Did us but loving wrong.
Did us only affectionate wrong.

MIRANDA
Alack, what trouble
What a shame, what trouble
Was I then to you!
I was then for you!

PROSPERO
O, a cherubim
Oh, little angel
Thou wast that did preserve me. Thou didst smile.
You were what saved me. You made me smile.
Infused with a fortitude from heaven,
Empowered with a strength from heaven,
When I have deck'd the sea with drops full salt,

When I crossed the salty sea,
Under my burthen groan'd; which raised in me
And groaned under my burden; it was that strength which raised in me
An undergoing stomach, to bear up
A continuous courage, to withstand
Against what should ensue.
What was to come.

MIRANDA
How came we ashore?
How did we come ashore?

PROSPERO
By Providence divine.
By Divine Providence.
Some food we had and some fresh water that
We had some food and some fresh water that
A noble Neapolitan, Gonzalo,
A noble man from Naples, named Gonzalo,
Out of his charity, being then appointed
Out of his kindness, having been put
Master of this design, did give us, with
In charge of this plan, gave to us, with
Rich garments, linens, stuffs and necessaries,
Nice clothes, linens, equipment and necessary things,
Which since have steaded much; so, of his gentleness,
Which have since been very helpful; so, because of his nobility,
Knowing I loved my books, he furnish'd me
And knowing that I loved my books, he provided me
From mine own library with volumes that
With books from my own library that
I prize above my dukedom.
I prized more than my dukedom.

MIRANDA
Would I might
I wish that I might
But ever see that man!
Someday see that man!

PROSPERO
Now I arise:
Now I will stand up:

Resumes his mantle (cloak)

Sit still, and hear the last of our sea-sorrow.
Sit still, and listen to the last of our sad times at sea.
Here in this island we arrived; and here
We arrived here on this island; and here
Have I, thy schoolmaster, made thee more profit
I have, as your school teacher, made you more capable
Than other princesses can that have more time
Than other princesses who have more time
For vainer hours and tutors not so careful.
To be foolishly spent and tutors who are not so careful.

MIRANDA

Heavens thank you for't! And now, I pray you, sir,
And the heavens thank you for it! And now, I ask you, sir,
For still 'tis beating in my mind, your reason
Because it's still heavy on my mind, what was your reason
For raising this sea-storm?
For raising this sea-storm?

PROSPERO

Know thus far forth.
Know this much.
By accident most strange, bountiful Fortune,
By a strange accident, from generous Fortune,
Now my dear lady, hath mine enemies
Now my dear lady, my enemies have been
Brought to this shore; and by my prescience
Brought to this shore; and because of my knowledge beforehand
I find my zenith doth depend upon
I found my high point depends on
A most auspicious star, whose influence
A very favorable star, which
If now I court not but omit, my fortunes
If I don't follow its influence now, but instead disregard it, my fortune
Will ever after droop. Here cease more questions:
Will fade forever after. Now stop more questionsL
Thou art inclined to sleep; 'tis a good dulness,
You are wishing to sleep; it's a good sleepiness,
And give it way: I know thou canst not choose.
And give in to it: I know you cannot do otherwise.

MIRANDA sleeps

Come away, servant, come. I am ready now.
Come here, servant, come. I am ready now.
Approach, my Ariel, come.
Approach, my Ariel come.

Enter ARIEL

ARIEL
All hail, great master! grave sir, hail! I come
Greetings, great master! Wise sir, greetings! I have come
To answer thy best pleasure; be't to fly,
To satisfy your dearest desire; whether it be to fly,
To swim, to dive into the fire, to ride
To swim, to dive into the fire, to ride
On the curl'd clouds, to thy strong bidding task
On the spiraling clouds, with your powerful commands, order
Ariel and all his quality.
Ariel and all of his companions.

PROSPERO
Hast thou, spirit,
Have you, spirit,
Perform'd to point the tempest that I bade thee?
Performed the tempest exactly as I commanded you?

ARIEL
To every article.
To the letter.
I boarded the king's ship; now on the beak,
I boarded the king's ship; first at the bow,
Now in the waist, the deck, in every cabin,
Then in the middle, the desk, in every cabin,
I flamed amazement: sometime I'ld divide,
I excited wonder and fear: sometimes I would separate,
And burn in many places; on the topmast,
And burn in many places; on the topmast,
The yards and bowsprit, would I flame distinctly,
The yards and bowsprit, I would excite them separately,
Then meet and join. Jove's lightnings, the precursors
Then meet and rejoin. The thunder god's lightning-bolts, the precursors
O' the dreadful thunder-claps, more momentary
Of the terrible thunder-claps, more fleeting
And sight-outrunning were not; the fire and cracks

And faster than the eye could follow weren't there; with fire and the booming
Of sulphurous roaring the most mighty Neptune
Of thunderous roaring the most mighty sea god
Seem to besiege and make his bold waves tremble,
Seemed to over take them and make his daring waves tremble,
Yea, his dread trident shake.
Oh yes, he shook his frightening trident.

PROSPERO
My brave spirit!
My excellent spirit!
Who was so firm, so constant, that this coil
Was there anyone who was so steadfast, so constant, that this tumult
Would not infect his reason?
Would not spoil his good sense?

ARIEL
Not a soul
Not a soul
But felt a fever of the mad and play'd
Instead they felt a fever like the mad and showed
Some tricks of desperation. All but mariners
Some characteristics of despair. All but the sailors
Plunged in the foaming brine and quit the vessel,
Jumped into the frothy sea water and left the ship.
Then all afire with me: the king's son, Ferdinand,
Then all on fire from me: the king's son, Ferdinand,
With hair up-staring,--then like reeds, not hair,--
With his hair standing on end,--more like reeds than hair,--
Was the first man that leap'd; cried, 'Hell is empty
Was the first man to leap overboard; he cried, 'Hell is empty
And all the devils are here.'
Because all the devils are here.'

PROSPERO
Why that's my spirit!
Well, that's my good servant!
But was not this nigh shore?
But wasn't this near shore?

ARIEL
Close by, my master.
Close by, my master.

PROSPERO
But are they, Ariel, safe?
But are they safe, Ariel?

ARIEL
Not a hair perish'd;
Not a single one died;
On their sustaining garments not a blemish,
Not even a stain on the clothes that saved them,
But fresher than before: and, as thou badest me,
But instead cleaner than before: and, as you asked me,
In troops I have dispersed them 'bout the isle.
I have dispersed them in groups around the island.
The king's son have I landed by himself;
The king's son I have brought to land by himself;
Whom I left cooling of the air with sighs
I left him blowing in the air with his sighs
In an odd angle of the isle and sitting,
In an odd corner of the island and sitting,
His arms in this sad knot.
His arms in a dejected knot.

PROSPERO
Of the king's ship
Of the king's ship and its
The mariners say how thou hast disposed
Sailor, tell me how you managed them
And all the rest o' the fleet.
And all the rest of the fleet.

ARIEL
Safely in harbour
Safely in the harbor
Is the king's ship; in the deep nook, where once
Is the king's ship; in a deep nook, where you once
Thou call'dst me up at midnight to fetch dew
Called me up at midnight to fetch dew
From the still-vex'd Bermoothes, there she's hid:
From the always stormy Bermuda, it's there that the ship is hidden:
The mariners all under hatches stow'd;
The sailors are all stowed under the decks;
Who, with a charm join'd to their suffer'd labour,
Who, with a spell combined with their hard work,
I have left asleep; and for the rest o' the fleet

I have left asleep; and for the rest of the fleet
Which I dispersed, they all have met again
Which I dispersed, they all have met up again
And are upon the Mediterranean flote,
And are floating on the Mediterranean,
Bound sadly home for Naples,
Sadly heading home for Naples,
Supposing that they saw the king's ship wreck'd
Thinking that they saw the king's whip wreckd
And his great person perish.
And his royalty perish.

PROSPERO
Ariel, thy charge
Ariel, you task
Exactly is perform'd: but there's more work.
Has been performed exactly: but there's more work.
What is the time o' the day?
What time of day is it?

ARIEL
Past the mid season.
Past noon.

PROSPERO
At least two glasses. The time 'twixt six and now
At least two hourglasses. The time between now and six
Must by us both be spent most preciously.
Must be spent most usefully for the both of us.

ARIEL
Is there more toil? Since thou dost give me pains,
Is there more work? Since you are giving me more tasks,
Let me remember thee what thou hast promised,
Let me remind you what you have promised,
Which is not yet perform'd me.
Which has not yet been given to me.

PROSPERO
How now? moody?
What's this? Are you angry?
What is't thou canst demand?
What is it you can ask for?

ARIEL
My liberty.
My freedom.

PROSPERO
Before the time be out? no more!
Before the time is up? Certainly not!

ARIEL
I prithee,
I ask you to
Remember I have done thee worthy service;
Remember that I have done excellent work for you;
Told thee no lies, made thee no mistakings, served
I have told you no lies, made you no mistakes, served you
Without or grudge or grumblings: thou didst promise
Without complaining or grumbling: you did promise
To bate me a full year.
To lessen my term by a whole year.

PROSPERO
Dost thou forget
Did you forget
From what a torment I did free thee?
What a torment I freed you from?

ARIEL
No.
No.

PROSPERO
Thou dost, and think'st it much to tread the ooze
You have, and think that it's too much to walk the bottom
Of the salt deep,
Of the sea,
To run upon the sharp wind of the north,
To run on the sharp north wind,
To do me business in the veins o' the earth
To do my tasks in the depths of the earth
When it is baked with frost.
When it is hardened with frost.

ARIEL
I do not, sir.

I do not, sir.

PROSPERO
Thou liest, malignant thing! Hast thou forgot
You are lying, you wicked thing! Have you forgotten
The foul witch Sycorax, who with age and envy
The terrible witch Sycorax, who this age and malice
Was grown into a hoop? hast thou forgot her?
Had grown into a hunchback? Have you forgotten her?

ARIEL
No, sir.
No, sir.

PROSPERO
Thou hast. Where was she born? speak; tell me.
You have. Where was she born? Speak up; tell me.

ARIEL
Sir, in Argier.
Sir, in Algiers.

PROSPERO
O, was she so? I must
Oh, was she? I must
Once in a month recount what thou hast been,
Once a month tell you what you have been,
Which thou forget'st. This damn'd witch Sycorax,
Which you forget. That damned witch Sycorax,
For mischiefs manifold and sorceries terrible
For many wicked deeds and terrible magic
To enter human hearing, from Argier,
That came into human hearing,
Thou know'st, was banish'd: for one thing she did
You know, was banished from Algiers; for one thing she did, becoming pregnant,
They would not take her life. Is not this true?
They would not take her life. Isn't that true?

ARIEL
Ay, sir.
Yes, sir.

PROSPERO
This blue-eyed hag was hither brought with child

That pregnant hag was brought here with child
And here was left by the sailors. Thou, my slave,
And was left here by the sailors. You, my servant,
As thou report'st thyself, wast then her servant;
As you had said yourself, were her servant then;
And, for thou wast a spirit too delicate
And, because you were a spirit too superb in nature
To act her earthy and abhorr'd commands,
To act out her mundane and horrifying commands,
Refusing her grand hests, she did confine thee,
For refusing her grand orders, she did imprison you,
By help of her more potent ministers
With the help go her more powerful helpers
And in her most unmitigable rage,
And in a very ruthless rage,
Into a cloven pine; within which rift
In a pine tree that was split apart; trapped with that split
Imprison'd thou didst painfully remain
You painfully remained
A dozen years; within which space she died
A dozen years; within that time she died
And left thee there; where thou didst vent thy groans
And left you there; where you did express your groans
As fast as mill-wheels strike. Then was this island—
As fast as a mill's water wheel turns. At that time, this island—
Save for the son that she did litter here,
Except for the son that she birthed here,
A freckled whelp hag-born--not honour'd with
A freckled pup born from a witch—was not graced with
A human shape.
A human being.

ARIEL
Yes, Caliban her son.
Yes, Caliban her son.

PROSPERO
Dull thing, I say so; he, that Caliban
A sullen boy, if I say so; he, that Caliban
Whom now I keep in service. Thou best know'st
Who I now keep as a slave. You had best remember
What torment I did find thee in; thy groans
The torment that I found you in; your groans
Did make wolves howl and penetrate the breasts

Made wolves howl and pieced the hearts
Of ever angry bears: it was a torment
Of always angry bears: it was the kind of torment
To lay upon the damn'd, which Sycorax
To sentence on the damned, which Sycorax
Could not again undo: it was mine art,
Couldn't again undo: it was my magic,
When I arrived and heard thee, that made gape
When I arrived here and heard you, that opened
The pine and let thee out.
The pine and let you out.

ARIEL
I thank thee, master.
Thank you, master.

PROSPERO
If thou more murmur'st, I will rend an oak
If you complain more, I will split open an oak
And peg thee in his knotty entrails till
And fasten you into it's knotted insides until
Thou hast howl'd away twelve winters.
You have howled for twelve years.

ARIEL
Pardon, master;
Forgive me, master;
I will be correspondent to command
I will comply to your command
And do my spiriting gently.
And to my spirit activities tamely.

PROSPERO
Do so, and after two days
Do that, and after two days
I will discharge thee.
I will free you.

ARIEL
That's my noble master!
That's my noble master!
What shall I do? say what; what shall I do?
What will I do? Tell me; what will I do?

PROSPERO

Go make thyself like a nymph o' the sea: be subject
Go make yourself like a nymph of the sea; be visible
To no sight but thine and mine, invisible
To no sight but yours and mine, invisible
To every eyeball else. Go take this shape
To every other eyeball. Go take this shape
And hither come in't: go, hence with diligence!
And come here in it: go, away with care!

Exit ARIEL

Awake, dear heart, awake! thou hast slept well; Awake!
Awake, dear heart, awake! You have slept well; awake!

MIRANDA

The strangeness of your story put
The strangeness of your story made
Heaviness in me.
Me sleepy.

PROSPERO

Shake it off. Come on;
Shake it of. Come on;
We'll visit Caliban my slave, who never
We'll visit Caliban, my slave, who never
Yields us kind answer.
Gives us a friendly answer.

MIRANDA

'Tis a villain, sir,
He's a scoundrel, sir,
I do not love to look on.
That I don't like to look at.

PROSPERO

But, as 'tis,
But, as it is,
We cannot miss him: he does make our fire,
We cannot do without him: he makes our fire,
Fetch in our wood and serves in offices
Brings in our wood, and serves in tasks
That profit us. What, ho! slave! Caliban!

That helps us. Hello! Slave! Caliban!
Thou earth, thou! speak.
You piece of dirt, you! Speak up.

CALIBAN
[Within] There's wood enough within.
[Inside] There's enough wood inside.

PROSPERO
Come forth, I say! there's other business for thee:
Come out, I say! There's other work for you:
Come, thou tortoise! when?
Come out, you tortoise! When will you come out?

Re-enter ARIEL like a water-nymph

Fine apparition! My quaint Ariel,
An excellent illusion! My clever Ariel,
Hark in thine ear.
Listen with your ears.

ARIEL
My lord it shall be done.
My lord it will be done.

Exit

PROSPERO
Thou poisonous slave, got by the devil himself
You poisonous slave, father by the devil himself
Upon thy wicked dam, come forth!
From your wicked mother, come out!

Enter CALIBAN

CALIBAN
As wicked dew as e'er my mother brush'd
May a dew as wicked as any my mother ever brushed
With raven's feather from unwholesome fen
With a raven's feather from a poisonous swamp
Drop on you both! a south-west blow on ye
Drop on both of you! May a south-west wind blow on you
And blister you all o'er!
And burn you all over!

PROSPERO

For this, be sure, to-night thou shalt have cramps,
Of this be sure, tonight you will have cramps,
Side-stitches that shall pen thy breath up; urchins
Side-stitches that will hold in your breath; goblins
Shall, for that vast of night that they may work,
Will, during that empty time of the night when they work,
All exercise on thee; thou shalt be pinch'd
All practice on you; you will be pinched
As thick as honeycomb, each pinch more stinging
As densely as the densest honeycomb, each pinch stinging more
Than bees that made 'em.
Than the bees that made them.

CALIBAN

I must eat my dinner.
I must eat my dinner.
This island's mine, by Sycorax my mother,
This island is mine, from Sycorax my mother,
Which thou takest from me. When thou camest first,
That you take from me. When you first came here,
Thou strokedst me and madest much of me, wouldst give me
You stroked me and made a fuss over me, you would give me
Water with berries in't, and teach me how
Water with berries in it, and teach me how
To name the bigger light, and how the less,
To name the big light of sun, and how smaller lights of the moon and stars,
That burn by day and night: and then I loved thee
That burn by day and night: and then I loved you
And show'd thee all the qualities o' the isle,
And showed you all the features of the island,
The fresh springs, brine-pits, barren place and fertile:
The fresh springs, the salt-pits, the barren places and fertile places:
Cursed be I that did so! All the charms
It's a cursed thing that I did so! May all the spells
Of Sycorax, toads, beetles, bats, light on you!
Of Sycorax, toads, beetles, bats, land on you!
For I am all the subjects that you have,
Because I am the only subject you have,
Which first was mine own king: and here you sty me
I, who was first my own king: and here you coop me up
In this hard rock, whiles you do keep from me

In this hard rock, while you keep me away from
The rest o' the island.
The rest of the island.

PROSPERO
Thou most lying slave,
You terrible lyring slave,
Whom stripes may move, not kindness! I have used thee,
A whipping may move you but not kindness! I have used you,
Filth as thou art, with human care, and lodged thee
Filth that you are, with human care, and housed you
In mine own cell, till thou didst seek to violate
In my own cell, until you tried to violate
The honour of my child.
My daughter's virginity.

CALIBAN
O ho, O ho! would't had been done!
Oh-ho, oh-ho! It would have been done!
Thou didst prevent me; I had peopled else
You stopped me; I would have populated the whole
This isle with Calibans.
Island with Calibans.

PROSPERO
Abhorred slave,
Disgusting slave,
Which any print of goodness wilt not take,
Who will not take any impression of goodness,
Being capable of all ill! I pitied thee,
Being only open to evil! I pitied you,
Took pains to make thee speak, taught thee each hour
Worked hard to make you speak, taught you every hour
One thing or other: when thou didst not, savage,
One thing or another: when you did not, savage,
Know thine own meaning, but wouldst gabble like
Know what you were saying, but would instead babble like
A thing most brutish, I endow'd thy purposes
A brutish creature, I enriched your goals
With words that made them known. But thy vile race,
With words that made them understandable. But you ugly creature,
Though thou didst learn, had that in't which good natures
Although you did learn, you had in you that which good natures
Could not abide to be with; therefore wast thou

Could not stand to be with; thus you were
Deservedly confined into this rock,
Justifiably confined to this rock,
Who hadst deserved more than a prison.
You who deserved more than a prison.

CALIBAN
You taught me language; and my profit on't
You taught me language; and what I gained from that
Is, I know how to curse. The red plague rid you
Is that I know how to curse. May the red plague kill you
For learning me your language!
For teaching me your language!

PROSPERO
Hag-seed, hence!
Witch-child, come here!
Fetch us in fuel; and be quick, thou'rt best,
Bring us in some fuel; and be quick, you are better
To answer other business. Shrug'st thou, malice?
When you're working on other tasks. Do you shrug, beast?
If thou neglect'st or dost unwillingly
If you are neglectful or are unwilling to do
What I command, I'll rack thee with old cramps,
What I command, I'll trouble you with loads of cramps,
Fill all thy bones with aches, make thee roar
Fill all of your bones with ahces, make you roar with pain
That beasts shall tremble at thy din.
So that beasts will tremble at your noise.

CALIBAN
No, pray thee.
No, please.
[Aside] I must obey: his art is of such power,
[Aside] I must obey him: his magic is of such power that
It would control my dam's god, Setebos,
it could overpower my mother's god, Setebos,
and make a vassal of him.
And turn him into a servant.

PROSPERO
So, slave; hence!
So, slave; go to work!

Exit CALIBAN

Re-enter ARIEL, invisible, playing and singing; FERDINAND following

ARIEL'S song.
Come unto these yellow sands,
Come onto these yellow sands,
And then take hands:
And then join hands:
Courtsied when you have and kiss'd
Curtsy when you have and kiss
The wild waves whist,
The silent wild wave,
Foot it featly here and there;
Dance away nimbly here and there;
And, sweet sprites, the burthen bear.
And, sweet spirits, bear the burden.
Hark, hark!
Listen, listen!
(Burthen dispersedly, within)
(Chorus from various places, inside)
The watch-dogs bark!
The watch-dogs bark!
(Burthen Bow-wow)
(Chorus barks)
Hark, hark! I hear
Listen, listen! I hear
The strain of strutting chanticleer
The sound of a strutting rooster
Cry, Cock-a-diddle-dow.
Crying, cock-a-doodle-doo.

FERDINAND
Where should this music be? i' the air or the earth?
Where is this music coming form? In the air or the earth?
It sounds no more: and sure, it waits upon
I don't here any more: and I'm sure it accompanies
Some god o' the island. Sitting on a bank,
Some god of the island. Sitting on the shore,
Weeping again the king my father's wreck,
Weeping because of the my father, the king's, wreck,
This music crept by me upon the waters,
This music crept up to me on the waters,
Allaying both their fury and my passion

Quelling both the fury of the waves and my passion
With its sweet air: thence I have follow'd it,
With its sweet melody: I have followed it here,
Or it hath drawn me rather. But 'tis gone.
Or rather it has lead me. But it's gone.
No, it begins again.
No, it begins again.

ARIEL sings
Full fathom five thy father lies;
Five whole fathoms down your father lies;
Of his bones are coral made;
His bones are made of coral;
Those are pearls that were his eyes:
The pearls that were his eyes:
Nothing of him that doth fade
All the parts of him that decay
But doth suffer a sea-change
Endure a change from the sea
Into something rich and strange.
Into something rich and strange.
Sea-nymphs hourly ring his knell
Sea-nymphs ring his funeral bell each hour
(Burthen Ding-dong)
(Chorus ding-dong)
Hark! now I hear them,--Ding-dong, bell.
Listen! Now I hear them,--ding-dong, the bell.

FERDINAND
The ditty does remember my drown'd father.
The song remembers my drowned father.
This is no mortal business, nor no sound
This is not the work of a mortal, nor is it a sound
That the earth owes. I hear it now above me.
That the earth possesses. I hear it now above me.

PROSPERO
The fringed curtains of thine eye advance
Your eyelids raise
And say what thou seest yond.
And tell me what you see over there.

MIRANDA
What is't? a spirit?

What is it? A spirit?
Lord, how it looks about! Believe me, sir,
Lord, how it looks around! Believe me, sir,
It carries a brave form. But 'tis a spirit.
It carries itself like a brave man. But it's a spirit.

PROSPERO
No, wench; it eats and sleeps and hath such senses
No, girl: it eats and sleeps and has the same senses
As we have, such. This gallant which thou seest
That we have. This gentleman that you see
Was in the wreck; and, but he's something stain'd
Was in the wreck; and, except that he's a little stained
With grief that's beauty's canker, thou mightst call him
With grief, which is the disease of beauty, you might call him
A goodly person: he hath lost his fellows
A good person: he has lost his comrades
And strays about to find 'em.
And wanders around to find them.

MIRANDA
I might call him
I might call him
A thing divine, for nothing natural
A thing of the gods, for nothing mortal
I ever saw so noble.
Have I ever see that was so noble.

PROSPERO
[Aside] It goes on, I see,
[Aside] it goes on, I see,
As my soul prompts it. Spirit, fine spirit! I'll free thee
As I suggest it. Sprit, excellent spirit! I'll free you
Within two days for this.
Within two days for this.

FERDINAND
Most sure, the goddess
I'm sure, this is the goddess
On whom these airs attend! Vouchsafe my prayer
That the song is following! Grant my request
May know if you remain upon this island;
To know if you live on this island;
And that you will some good instruction give

And that you will give me some good instruction
How I may bear me here: my prime request,
On how I can sustain myself here: my main request,
Which I do last pronounce, is, O you wonder!
Which I do ask last, is—oh you beauty!--
If you be maid or no?
Are you a lady or no?

MIRANDA
No wonder, sir;
Don't wonder, sir;
But certainly a maid.
But certainly I am a lady.

FERDINAND
My language! heavens!
My word! Good heavens!
I am the best of them that speak this speech,
I am the highest ranking person of them all who speak this language,
Were I but where 'tis spoken.
If I were only where this language was spoken.

PROSPERO
How? the best?
How so? The highest ranking?
What wert thou, if the King of Naples heard thee?
What would you be if the King of Naples head you say that?

FERDINAND
A single thing, as I am now, that wonders
The same thing I am now, that marvels
To hear thee speak of Naples. He does hear me;
To hear you speak of Naples. The King of Naples does hear me;
And that he does I weep: myself am Naples,
And that his spirit can, causes me to weep: I am now the ruler of Naples,
Who with mine eyes, never since at ebb, beheld
Who with my own eyes, which haven't closed since, saw
The king my father wreck'd.
The my father, the king's ship, wrecked.

MIRANDA
Alack, for mercy!
Such shame, such a pity!

FERDINAND
Yes, faith, and all his lords; the Duke of Milan
Yes, believe me, and all of his lords; the Duke of Milan
And his brave son being twain.
And his brave son being two of those.

PROSPERO
[Aside] The Duke of Milan
[Aside] The Duke of Milan
And his more braver daughter could control thee,
And his much braver daughter could control you,
If now 'twere fit to do't. At the first sight
If now was a good time to do it. At first sight
They have changed eyes. Delicate Ariel,
They have exchanged glances. Delicate Ariel,
I'll set thee free for this.
I'll set you free for this.

To FERDINAND

A word, good sir;
May I have a word with you, good sir;
I fear you have done yourself some wrong: a word.
I'm afraid you have done yourself some discredit: a word.

MIRANDA
Why speaks my father so ungently? This
What does my father speak so roughly? This
Is the third man that e'er I saw, the first
Is the third man that I've ever seen, the first
That e'er I sigh'd for: pity move my father
That I ever swooned for: may pity move my father
To be inclined my way!
To think the same as me!

FERDINAND
O, if a virgin,
Oh, if you are a virgin,
And your affection not gone forth, I'll make you
And do not live someone else, I'll make you
The queen of Naples.
The queen of Naples.

PROSPERO

Soft, sir! one word more.
Not so fast, sir! Another word.

[Aside] They are both in either's powers; but this swift business
[Aside] They are both in each other's power; but this quick business
I must uneasy make, lest too light winning
I must make hard, in case an easy win
Make the prize light.
Makes the prize worthless.

To FERDINAND

One word more; I charge thee
Another word; I ask you
That thou attend me: thou dost here usurp
To listen to me: you here took wrongful possession
The name thou owest not; and hast put thyself
Of a name you do not possess; and you have put yourself
Upon this island as a spy, to win it
On this island as a spy, to win it
From me, the lord on't.
From me, the lord of the island.

FERDINAND
No, as I am a man.
No, as surely as I am a man I swear that's not true.

MIRANDA
There's nothing ill can dwell in such a temple:
There's nothing bad than can live in such a body:
If the ill spirit have so fair a house,
If a bad spirit had such a beautiful body,
Good things will strive to dwell with't.
Good things would try and live with it.

PROSPERO
Follow me.
Follow me.
Speak not you for him; he's a traitor. Come;
Don't speak for him; he's a traitor. Come one;
I'll manacle thy neck and feet together:
I'll chain your neck and feet together:
Sea-water shalt thou drink; thy food shall be

You will drink salt water; your food will be
The fresh-brook muscles, wither'd roots and husks
Muscles from the fresh streams, withered roots, and shells
Wherein the acorn cradled. Follow.
That once held acorns. Follow me.

FERDINAND
No;
No;
I will resist such entertainment till
I will resist such treatment until
Mine enemy has more power.
My enemy has more power.

[Draws, and is charmed from moving]
"[He draws his sword, and his magically charmed from moving]"

MIRANDA
O dear father,
Oh, dear father.
Make not too rash a trial of him, for
Don't make an impulsive judgment of him, because
He's gentle and not fearful.
He's gentle and not terrifying.

PROSPERO
What? I say,
What's this? I say,
My foot my tutor? Put thy sword up, traitor;
Someone beneath me as my teacher? Put away your sword, traitor;
Who makest a show but darest not strike, thy conscience
You who make a show but don't dare strike, your conscience
Is so possess'd with guilt: come from thy ward,
Is so overcome with guilt: come out of your defensive stance,
For I can here disarm thee with this stick
As I can disarm you here with a stick
And make thy weapon drop.
And make your weapon fall.

MIRANDA
Beseech you, father.
I beg you, father.

PROSPERO

Hence! hang not on my garments.
Stand back! Don't hang on my clothes.

MIRANDA
Sir, have pity;
Sir, have pity;
I'll be his surety.
I'll assure you of his goodness.

PROSPERO
Silence! one word more
Silence! If you say another word
Shall make me chide thee, if not hate thee. What!
I will scold you, if I don't hate you. What!
An advocate for an imposter! hush!
A defender for this imposter! Hush!
Thou think'st there is no more such shapes as he,
Do you think there is no one else who looks as handsome as him,
Having seen but him and Caliban: foolish wench!
Having only seen him and Caliban: foolish girl!
To the most of men this is a Caliban
To most men this is an ugly man like Caliban
And they to him are angels.
And they are like angels compared to him.

MIRANDA
My affections
My feelings
Are then most humble; I have no ambition
Then are very modest; I have no desire
To see a goodlier man.
To see a better-looking man.

PROSPERO
Come on; obey:
Come on; obey me:
Thy nerves are in their infancy again
Your muscles are like a baby's again
And have no vigour in them.
And have no power in them.

FERDINAND
So they are;

So they are;
My spirits, as in a dream, are all bound up.
My thoughts are all tied up, like in a dream.
My father's loss, the weakness which I feel,
The loss of my father, the weakness that I feel,
The wreck of all my friends, nor this man's threats,
The wreck of all my friends, not even this man's threats,
To whom I am subdued, are but light to me,
Who has overpowered me, are just minor things to me.
Might I but through my prison once a day
If I might just through the bars of my prison once a day
Behold this maid: all corners else o' the earth
See this lady: all other corners of the earth
Let liberty make use of; space enough
Freedom can have; I will have enough space
Have I in such a prison.
In such a prison.

PROSPERO
[Aside] It works.
[Aside] It's working.

To FERDINAND

Come on.
Come on.
Thou hast done well, fine Ariel!
[Aside] You have done well, fine Ariel!

To FERDINAND

Follow me.
Follow me.

To ARIEL

Hark what thou else shalt do me.
Listen to what else you will do for me.

MIRANDA
Be of comfort;
Take comfort;
My father's of a better nature, sir,

My father's a better man, sir,
Than he appears by speech: this is unwonted
Than he seems to be from this talk: this is unusual
Which now came from him.
What just now came from him.

PROSPERO
Thou shalt be free
You shall be free
As mountain winds: but then exactly do
As the mountain wind: but you must exactly do
All points of my command.
Ever little thing I command.

ARIEL
To the syllable.
I will do it to the letter.

PROSPERO
Come, follow. Speak not for him.
Come on, follow me. Don't speak for him.

Exeunt

ACT II

SCENE I.
Another part of the island.
Enter ALONSO, SEBASTIAN, ANTONIO, GONZALO, ADRIAN, FRANCISCO, and others

GONZALO
Beseech you, sir, be merry; you have cause,
I ask you, sir, to be happy; you have a reason,
So have we all, of joy; for our escape
So do we all, for joy; because the fact that we escaped
Is much beyond our loss. Our hint of woe
Is much greater than our loss. Our experience of sadness
Is common; every day some sailor's wife,
Is common; every day some sailor's wife,
The masters of some merchant and the merchant
The sea-captains of some merchant-ship and the merchant himself
Have just our theme of woe; but for the miracle,

Have the same experience of sadness; except for the miracle,
I mean our preservation, few in millions
I mean our escape, only a few in millions
Can speak like us: then wisely, good sir, weigh
Come out as well as we have: so wisely, good sir, weigh
Our sorrow with our comfort.
Our sorrow with our relief.

ALONSO
Prithee, peace.
Please, be silent.

SEBASTIAN
He receives comfort like cold porridge.
He receives comfort like cold porridge.

ANTONIO
The visitor will not give him o'er so.
The comforter will not leave him like this.

SEBASTIAN
Look he's winding up the watch of his wit;
Look, he's thinking about what to say;
by and by it will strike.
And soon he will speak.

GONZALO
Sir,--
Sir,--

SEBASTIAN
One: tell.
There's one: count it.

GONZALO
When every grief is entertain'd that's offer'd,
When every grief that happens is let in,
Comes to the entertainer—
There comes over the recipient--

SEBASTIAN
A dollar.
That's a dollar's worth.

GONZALO

Dolour comes to him, indeed: you
Sorrow comes to him, indeed: you
have spoken truer than you purposed.
Have spoken more truthfully than you intended.

SEBASTIAN

You have taken it wiselier than I meant you should.
You have taken it more sensibly than I meant for you to.

GONZALO

Therefore, my lord,--
So, my lord,--

ANTONIO

Fie, what a spendthrift is he of his tongue!
Nonsense, he doesn't waste words!

ALONSO

I prithee, spare.
Please, spare me.

GONZALO

Well, I have done: but yet,--
Well, I have: but still,--

SEBASTIAN

He will be talking.
He keeps talking.

ANTONIO

Which, of he or Adrian, for a good
Which do you think, between him or Adrian, for a nice
wager, first begins to crow?
Bet, will first begin to complain?

SEBASTIAN

The old cock.
The old man.

ANTONIO

The cockerel.
The young one.

SEBASTIAN
Done. The wager?
Done. What's the bet?

ANTONIO
A laughter.
A good laugh.

SEBASTIAN
A match!
We have a deal!

ADRIAN
Though this island seem to be desert,--
But this island seems to be a desert,--

SEBASTIAN
Ha, ha, ha! So, you're paid.
Ha, ha, ha! So, you won.

ADRIAN
Uninhabitable and almost inaccessible,--
Uninhabitable and almost inaccessible,--

SEBASTIAN
Yet,--
But,--

ADRIAN
Yet,--
But,--

ANTONIO
He could not miss't.
He couldn't miss it.

ADRIAN
It must needs be of subtle, tender and delicate
It seems to be of a nice, gentle and pleasant
temperance.
Climate.

ANTONIO
Temperance was a delicate wench.

Climate is a self-indulgent girl.

SEBASTIAN
Ay, and a subtle; as he most learnedly delivered.
Yes, and a fine one; as he very intelligently said.

ADRIAN
The air breathes upon us here most sweetly.
The air blows on us here very sweetly.

SEBASTIAN
As if it had lungs and rotten ones.
As if it had lungs, and bad ones.

ANTONIO
Or as 'twere perfumed by a fen.
Or if it used a swamp for perfume.

GONZALO
Here is everything advantageous to life.
There is everything here that is useful to life.

ANTONIO
True; save means to live.
True; except the necessary things to live.

SEBASTIAN
Of that there's none, or little.
Of that there's none, or little.

GONZALO
How lush and lusty the grass looks! how green!
How lush and strong the grass looks! How green!

ANTONIO
The ground indeed is tawny.
The ground is in fact a tan brown.

SEBASTIAN
With an eye of green in't.
With a hint of green in it.

ANTONIO
He misses not much.

He doesn't miss much.

SEBASTIAN
No; he doth but mistake the truth totally.
No; he just misses the truth completely.

GONZALO
But the rarity of it is,--which is indeed almost
But the exceptional part of it is,--which is infact almost
beyond credit,--
Beyond belief,--

SEBASTIAN
As many vouched rarities are.
As many certified rare things are.

GONZALO
That our garments, being, as they were, drenched in
That our clothes, having been soaked as they were in
the sea, hold notwithstanding their freshness and
The sea, nevertheless still are fresh and
glosses, being rather new-dyed than stained with
Shiny, seeming more like they have just been newly dyed instead of stained with
salt water.
Salt water.

ANTONIO
If but one of his pockets could speak, would it not
If just one of his pockets could speak, wouldn't it
say he lies?
Say that he's lying?

SEBASTIAN
Ay, or very falsely pocket up his report
Yes, or it would be wrongly accepting his insult.

GONZALO
Methinks our garments are now as fresh as when we
I think our clothes are now as clean as when we
put them on first in Afric, at the marriage of
First put them on in Africa, at the marriage of
the king's fair daughter Claribel to the King of Tunis.
The king's lovely daughter Claribel to the King of Tunis.

SEBASTIAN
'Twas a sweet marriage, and we prosper well in our return.
It was a sweet marriage, and we will prosper well when we return.

ADRIAN
Tunis was never graced before with such a paragon to
Tunis was never graced before with such a beauty as
their queen.
Their queen.

GONZALO
Not since widow Dido's time.
Not since the widow Dido's time.

ANTONIO
Widow! a pox o' that! How came that widow in?
Widow! Curse that! Why did you call her a widow?
widow Dido!
Widow Dido!

SEBASTIAN
What if he had said 'widower AEneas' too? Good Lord,
What if had also said, 'the widower Aeneas'? Good Lord,
how you take it!
How would you stand it!

ADRIAN
'Widow Dido' said you? you make me study of that:
You said, 'the widow Dido'? You made me think about that:
she was of Carthage, not of Tunis.
She was from Carthage, not from Tunis.

GONZALO
This Tunis, sir, was Carthage.
Tunis, sir, used to be Carthage.

ADRIAN
Carthage?
Carthage?

GONZALO
I assure you, Carthage.
I promise you, Carthage.

SEBASTIAN
His word is more than the miraculous harp; he hath
His word is greater than the magical harp that built the walls of Thebes; he has
raised the wall and houses too.
Built the wall and houses too.

ANTONIO
What impossible matter will he make easy next?
What impossible task will he make simple next?

SEBASTIAN
I think he will carry this island home in his pocket
I think he will carry this island home in his pocket
and give it his son for an apple.
And give it to his son as an apple.

ANTONIO
And, sowing the kernels of it in the sea, bring
And, by planting the seeds of it in the sea, he will
forth more islands.
Grow more islands.

GONZALO
Ay.
Yes.

ANTONIO
Why, in good time.
Well, all in good time.

GONZALO
Sir, we were talking that our garments seem now
Sir, we were talking about how our clothes now seem
as fresh as when we were at Tunis at the marriage
As clean as when we were in Tunis at the wedding
of your daughter, who is now queen.
Of your daughter, who is now queen.

ANTONIO
And the rarest that e'er came there.
And the most exceptional queen that ever was there.

SEBASTIAN
Bate, I beseech you, widow Dido.

Except, I tell you, the widow Dido.

ANTONIO
O, widow Dido! ay, widow Dido.
Oh, the widow Dido! Yes, the widow Dido.

GONZALO
Is not, sir, my doublet as fresh as the first day I
Sir, isn't my jacket as clean as the first day that I
wore it? I mean, in a sort.
Wore it? I mean, in a way.

ANTONIO
That sort was well fished for.
If you look hard for that 'way'.

GONZALO
When I wore it at your daughter's marriage?
When I wore it at your daughter's wedding?

ALONSO
You cram these words into mine ears against
You cram these words into my ears against
The stomach of my sense. Would I had never
What my mind wants. I wish I had never
Married my daughter there! for, coming thence,
Married my daughter there! For, in going there,
My son is lost and, in my rate, she too,
I have lost my son, and in my opinion, lost her too,
Who is so far from Italy removed
She is now so far away from Italy that
I ne'er again shall see her. O thou mine heir
I'll never see her again. Oh, my heir
Of Naples and of Milan, what strange fish
Of Naples and Milan, what strange fish
Hath made his meal on thee?
Have eaten your body in the sea?

FRANCISCO
Sir, he may live:
Sir, he may live:
I saw him beat the surges under him,
I saw him kick the waves under him,
And ride upon their backs; he trod the water,

And ride on their backs; he tread the water,
Whose enmity he flung aside, and breasted
Whose hostility he cast aside, and tackled
The surge most swoln that met him; his bold head
The giant wave that met him; he kept his bold head
'Bove the contentious waves he kept, and oar'd
Above the warring waves, and rowed
Himself with his good arms in lusty stroke
Himself with his good arms in strong strokes
To the shore, that o'er his wave-worn basis bow'd,
To the shore, and over its wave-worn sands he bowed,
As stooping to relieve him: I not doubt
as if he stooped to relieve himself: I don't doubt
He came alive to land.
That he got to land alive.

ALONSO
No, no, he's gone.
No, no, he's gone.

SEBASTIAN
Sir, you may thank yourself for this great loss,
Sir, you may blame yourself for this great loss,
That would not bless our Europe with your daughter,
That would take the blessing of your daughter away from Europe,
But rather lose her to an African;
and instead lose her to an African man;
Where she at least is banish'd from your eye,
Where at least she is out of your eyesight,
Who hath cause to wet the grief on't.
Your daughter who gave you reason for the tears of grief in your eyes.

ALONSO
Prithee, peace.
Please, silence.

SEBASTIAN
You were kneel'd to and importuned otherwise
You were begged and urged not to do this
By all of us, and the fair soul herself
By all of us, and the lovely girl herself
Weigh'd between loathness and obedience, at
Went back and forth between hatred and obedience, at
Which end o' the beam should bow. We have lost your

Whichever side of the scale was weighed down. We have lost your
son,
Son,
I fear, for ever: Milan and Naples have
Forever, I'm afraid: Milan and Naples have
More widows in them of this business' making
More widows in them due to this incident
Than we bring men to comfort them:
Than the number of men we could bring to comfort them:
The fault's your own.
It's your fault.

ALONSO
So is the dear'st o' the loss.
So is the worst of the loss.

GONZALO
My lord Sebastian,
My lord Sebastian,
The truth you speak doth lack some gentleness
The truth you speak lacks some tenderness
And time to speak it in: you rub the sore,
And the right time to bring it up: you're aggravating the wound
When you should bring the plaster.
When you should be trying to heal it.

SEBASTIAN
Very well.
Very well.

ANTONIO
And most chirurgeonly.
And quite like a doctor.

GONZALO
It is foul weather in us all, good sir,
It's bad news for us all, good sirm
When you are cloudy.
When you are saddened.

SEBASTIAN
Foul weather?
Bad news?

ANTONIO
Very foul.
Very bad.

GONZALO
Had I plantation of this isle, my lord,--
If I had a settlement on this island, my lord,--

ANTONIO
He'ld sow't with nettle-seed.
He would plant it with stinging nettles.

SEBASTIAN
Or docks, or mallows.
Or weeds, or wild plants.

GONZALO
And were the king on't, what would I do?
And I were the of it, what would I do?

SEBASTIAN
'Scape being drunk for want of wine.
Avoid being drunk from the lack of wine.

GONZALO
I' the commonwealth I would by contraries
In the nation I would very differently
Execute all things; for no kind of traffic
Run all things; no kind of trade
Would I admit; no name of magistrate;
Would I allow; I would name no officials;
Letters should not be known; riches, poverty,
Learning would not be known; riches, poverty,
And use of service, none; contract, succession,
And the use of slaves, none of that; contracts, inheritance,
Bourn, bound of land, tilth, vineyard, none;
Limits and boundaries of land, farms, vineyards, none of that;
No use of metal, corn, or wine, or oil;
No use of metal, corn, or wine, or oil;
No occupation; all men idle, all;
No trades; all men would be at leisure, all of them;
And women too, but innocent and pure;
And women too, but innocent and pure;
No sovereignty;--

No royalty;--

SEBASTIAN
Yet he would be king on't.
Yet he would be the king of it.

ANTONIO
The latter end of his commonwealth forgets the
This other end of his nation forgets the
beginning.
Beginning.

GONZALO
All things in common nature should produce
All things of a universal nature would produce
Without sweat or endeavour: treason, felony,
Without toil or work: treason, felony,
Sword, pike, knife, gun, or need of any engine,
Sword, pike, knife, gun, or need of any weapon,
Would I not have; but nature should bring forth,
I would not have; but nature would create,
Of its own kind, all foison, all abundance,
From itself, a great plenty, all abundance,
To feed my innocent people.
To feed my innocent people.

SEBASTIAN
No marrying 'mong his subjects?
So no marrying between his subjects?

ANTONIO
None, man; all idle: whores and knaves.
There would be none, man; they're all idle: whores and scoundrels.

GONZALO
I would with such perfection govern, sir,
I would govern with such perfection, sir,
To excel the golden age.
To bring about the golden age.

SEBASTIAN
God save his majesty!
God save his majesty!

ANTONIO
Long live Gonzalo!
Long live Gonzalo!

GONZALO
And,--do you mark me, sir?
An—are you listening to me, sir?

ALONSO
Prithee, no more: thou dost talk nothing to me.
Please, no more: you are saying nothing to me.

GONZALO
I do well believe your highness; and
I do believe this your highness; and
did it to minister occasion to these gentlemen,
I did it to supply the opportunity to these gentleman,
who are of such sensible and nimble lungs that
Who have such responsibe and quick lungs that
they always use to laugh at nothing.
They used to always laugh at nothing.

ANTONIO
'Twas you we laughed at.
It was you that we laughed at.

GONZALO
Who in this kind of merry fooling am nothing
In this kind of happy silliness I am nothing
to you: so you may continue and laugh at
To you: so you may continue and laugh at
nothing still.
Nothing still.

ANTONIO
What a blow was there given!
What a blow he just gave us!

SEBASTIAN
An it had not fallen flat-long.
And it didn't hit with the flat of the blde.

GONZALO
You are gentlemen of brave metal; you would lift

You are gentleman of noble resolve; you would lift
the moon out of her sphere, if she would continue
The moon out of her orbit, if she would keep
in it five weeks without changing.
It going for five weeks without changing.

Enter ARIEL, invisible, playing solemn music

SEBASTIAN
We would so, and then go a bat-fowling.
We would do so, and then go catch roosting birds at night.

ANTONIO
Nay, good my lord, be not angry.
No, my good lord, don't be angry.

GONZALO
No, I warrant you; I will not adventure
No, I assure you; I will not risk
my discretion so weakly. Will you laugh
My judgment with such weakness. Will you laugh
me asleep, for I am very heavy?
Me to sleep, for I am very sleepy?

ANTONIO
Go sleep, and hear us.
Go to sleep, and listen to us.

All sleep except ALONSO, SEBASTIAN, and ANTONIO

ALONSO
What, all so soon asleep! I wish mine eyes
Look at that, all so quickly asleep! I wish my eyes
Would, with themselves, shut up my thoughts: I find
Would, along with themselves, silence my thoughts: I find
They are inclined to do so.
They are inclined to do so.

SEBASTIAN
Please you, sir,
Please you, sir,
Do not omit the heavy offer of it:
Do not deny the pressing offer of sleep:
It seldom visits sorrow; when it doth,

It seldom visits sorrow: and with it does,
It is a comforter.
It is a comfort,

ANTONIO
We two, my lord,
My lord, we two
Will guard your person while you take your rest,
Will guard your person while you take tour rest,
And watch your safety.
And watch out for your safety.

ALONSO
Thank you. Wondrous heavy.
Thank you. Wondrous sleep.

ALONSO sleeps. Exit ARIEL

SEBASTIAN
What a strange drowsiness possesses them!
What a strange sleepiness

ANTONIO
It is the quality o' the climate.
It's a characteristic of the climate.

SEBASTIAN
Why
Why
Doth it not then our eyelids sink? I find not
Does it not lower our eyelids then? I don't find
Myself disposed to sleep.
Myself wanting to sleep.

ANTONIO
Nor I; my spirits are nimble.
Neither do I; my spirits are lively.
They fell together all, as by consent;
They all fell asleep together, as if in agreement;
They dropp'd, as by a thunder-stroke. What might,
They dropped down is if thunder-stuck. What might that be,
Worthy Sebastian? O, what might?--No more:--
Worthy Sebastian? Oh, what might it be?—I'll say no more:--
And yet me thinks I see it in thy face,

And yet I think I see it in your face,
What thou shouldst be: the occasion speaks thee, and
What you might be: the circumstance calls on you, and
My strong imagination sees a crown
My strong imagination sees a crown
Dropping upon thy head.
Dropping on to your head.

SEBASTIAN
What, art thou waking?
What, are you awake?

ANTONIO
Do you not hear me speak?
Don't you hear me speaking?

SEBASTIAN
I do; and surely
I do; and certainly
It is a sleepy language and thou speak'st
It's a dream-like language and you're speaking
Out of thy sleep. What is it thou didst say?
As if in your sleep. What did you say?
This is a strange repose, to be asleep
This is a strange rest, to be asleep
With eyes wide open; standing, speaking, moving,
With eyes wide open; standing speaking, moving,
And yet so fast asleep.
And still so fast asleep.

ANTONIO
Noble Sebastian,
Noble Sebastian,
Thou let'st thy fortune sleep--die, rather; wink'st
You let you're your fortune sleep—or die, rather; sleeping
Whiles thou art waking.
While you are awake.

SEBASTIAN
Thou dost snore distinctly;
You're certainly snoring;
There's meaning in thy snores.
There's meaning in your snores.

ANTONIO
I am more serious than my custom: you
I am more serious than usual: you
Must be so too, if heed me; which to do
Must be so too, if you follow me; which if you do
Trebles thee o'er.
Triples you.

SEBASTIAN
Well, I am standing water.
Well, I am at a stand still

ANTONIO
I'll teach you how to flow.
I'll teach you how to rise up.

SEBASTIAN
Do so: to ebb
Do so: to pull back
Hereditary sloth instructs me.
My inherited laziness teach me.

ANTONIO
O,
Oh,
If you but knew how you the purpose cherish
If you only know how you cherish the plan
Whiles thus you mock it! how, in stripping it,
While you are making fun of it! How, in shredding it up,
You more invest it! Ebbing men, indeed,
You invest more into it! Retreating men, indeed,
Most often do so near the bottom run
Do so most often near the last stretch
By their own fear or sloth.
From their own fear of laziness.

SEBASTIAN
Prithee, say on:
Please, continue:
The setting of thine eye and cheek proclaim
The settled look of your eye and cheek proclaim
A matter from thee, and a birth indeed
An important matter from you, and indeed a birth rank
Which throes thee much to yield.

Which tortures you a lot to reveal.

ANTONIO
Thus, sir:
So, sir:
Although this lord of weak remembrance, this,
Although lord Gonzalo of the poor memory, he
Who shall be of as little memory
Who will have just as poor of a memory
When he is earth'd, hath here almost persuade,--
When he is buried, has just almost persuaded,--
For he's a spirit of persuasion, only
Because he's a man of persuasion, only
Professes to persuade,--the king his son's alive,
Speaking in order to persuade,--the king that his son is alive,
'Tis as impossible that he's undrown'd
It's as impossible that he didn't drown
And he that sleeps here swims.
As it is for he who sleeps here is also swimming.

SEBASTIAN
I have no hope
I have no hope
That he's undrown'd.
That he didn't drown.

ANTONIO
O, out of that 'no hope'
Oh, and from that 'no hope'
What great hope have you! no hope that way is
What great hope you have! No hope in that way is in
Another way so high a hope that even
Another way a hope so high that even
Ambition cannot pierce a wink beyond,
Ambition cannot peak beyond,
But doubt discovery there. Will you grant with me
For fear of traveling there. Will you agree with me
That Ferdinand is drown'd?
That Ferdinand has drowned?

SEBASTIAN
He's gone.
He's dead.

ANTONIO
Then, tell me,
Then, tell me,
Who's the next heir of Naples?
Who's the next heir of Naples?

SEBASTIAN
Claribel.
Claribel.

ANTONIO
She that is queen of Tunis; she that dwells
She who is queen of Tunis; she who lives
Ten leagues beyond man's life; she that from Naples
Ten leagues away from civilized life; she who
Can have no note, unless the sun were post—
Can have no information from Naples, unless the sun carried the letter--
The man i' the moon's too slow--till new-born chins
The man in the moon is too slow—until the time it takes for babies chins
Be rough and razorable; she that from whom
Become rough and ready to shave; she who we travelled away from when
We all were sea-swallow'd, though some cast again,
We were all swallowed by the sea, though some were thrown out again,
And by that destiny to perform an act
And, because of that sequence of events, are now here to carry out an act
Whereof what's past is prologue, what to come
To which the past is only a prologue, what is to come
In yours and my discharge.
Is yours and my performance.

SEBASTIAN
What stuff is this! how say you?
What is this! What are you saying?
'Tis true, my brother's daughter's queen of Tunis;
It's true, my brother's daughter is queen of Tunis;
So is she heir of Naples; 'twixt which regions
She is also heir of Naples; between the two regions
There is some space.
There is some space.

ANTONIO
A space whose every cubit
A space whose every inch
Seems to cry out, 'How shall that Claribel

Seems to ask, 'How will Claribel
Measure us back to Naples? Keep in Tunis,
Trace us back to Naples? Stay in Tunis,
And let Sebastian wake.' Say, this were death
And let Sebastian wake.' What if this were death
That now hath seized them; why, they were no worse
That has now seized them; why, they would be no worse
Than now they are. There be that can rule Naples
Than they are now. There are those who can rule Naples
As well as he that sleeps; lords that can prate
As well as the man who is sleeping; lords that can blather
As amply and unnecessarily
As thoroughly and unnecessarily
As this Gonzalo; I myself could make
As this Gonzalo; I myself could make
A chough of as deep chat. O, that you bore
A crow of that kind of learned chatter. Oh, if only you had
The mind that I do! what a sleep were this
The mind that I do! What a sleep this would be
For your advancement! Do you understand me?
For your advancement! Do you understand me?

SEBASTIAN
Methinks I do.
I think I do.

ANTONIO
And how does your content
And how does you pleasure
Tender your own good fortune?
Regard you own good fortune?

SEBASTIAN
I remember
I remember
You did supplant your brother Prospero.
That you displaced your brother Prospero.

ANTONIO
True:
True:
And look how well my garments sit upon me;
And look how well my royal garb looks on me;
Much feater than before: my brother's servants

Much more well fitting than before: my brother's servants
Were then my fellows; now they are my men.
Were my companions then; now they are my servants.

SEBASTIAN
But, for your conscience?
But what about your conscience?

ANTONIO
Ay, sir; where lies that? if 'twere a kibe,
Yes, sir; where is that? If it were an inflammation on my heel,
'Twould put me to my slipper: but I feel not
It would force me to wear my slippers: but I don't feel
This deity in my bosom: twenty consciences,
This godliness in my heart: twenty consciences
That stand 'twixt me and Milan, candied be they
That would stand between me and Milan, may they be frozen
And melt ere they molest! Here lies your brother,
And melt away before they cause trouble! Here lies your brother,
No better than the earth he lies upon,
No better than the earth he's lying on,
If he were that which now he's like, that's dead;
If he were that which he now appears to be—that would be dead—
 Whom I, with this obedient steel, three inches of it,
I, with this obedient sword, three inches of it,
Can lay to bed for ever; whiles you, doing thus,
Could put him to sleep for ever; while you, doing as I show you,
To the perpetual wink for aye might put
To the eternal eyes shutting for ever might put
This ancient morsel, this Sir Prudence, who
This ancient mouthful, this Sir Prudence, who
Should not upbraid our course. For all the rest,
Will not stand against our actions. For all the others,
They'll take suggestion as a cat laps milk;
They'll take a hint like a cat drinks up milk;
They'll tell the clock to any business that
They'll tell the time on a clock to any matter that
We say befits the hour.
We say is fitting to the time.

SEBASTIAN
Thy case, dear friend,
Your situation, dear friend,
Shall be my precedent; as thou got'st Milan,

Will be my guide; as you got Milan,
I'll come by Naples. Draw thy sword: one stroke
I'll get Naples. Draw your sword: one stroke
Shall free thee from the tribute which thou payest;
Will free you from the taxes which you pay;
And I the king shall love thee.
And as the king I will love you.

ANTONIO
Draw together;
We'll draw them together;
And when I rear my hand, do you the like,
And when I raise my hand, you do the same,
To fall it on Gonzalo.
To bring it down on Gonzalo.

SEBASTIAN
O, but one word.
Oh, but one word.

They talk apart
Re-enter ARIEL, invisible

ARIEL
My master through his art foresees the danger
My master though his magic foresees the danger
That you, his friend, are in; and sends me forth—
That you, his friend, are in; and he sends me here--
For else his project dies--to keep them living.
To keep him living—because otherwise his project will fail.

Sings in GONZALO's ear

While you here do snoring lie,
While you lie here snoring,
Open-eyed conspiracy
Open-eyed conspiracy
His time doth take.
Finds the right moment.
If of life you keep a care,
If you care to keep your life,
Shake off slumber, and beware:
Shake off this sleep, and beware:
Awake, awake!

Awake, awake!

ANTONIO
Then let us both be sudden.
The let us both be quick.

GONZALO
Now, good angels
Now, good angels
Preserve the king.
Save the king.

They wake

ALONSO
Why, how now? ho, awake! Why are you drawn?
Why, what's this? Hello, awake! Why are your swords drawn?
Wherefore this ghastly looking?
Why his frightened look?

GONZALO
What's the matter?
What's the matter?

SEBASTIAN
Whiles we stood here securing your repose,
While we stood here guarding your rest,
Even now, we heard a hollow burst of bellowing
Just now, we heard an echoing burst of bellowing
Like bulls, or rather lions: did't not wake you?
Like bulls, or maybe lions: didn't it wake you?
It struck mine ear most terribly.
It hit my ear terribly.

ALONSO
I heard nothing.
I heard nothing.

ANTONIO
O, 'twas a din to fright a monster's ear,
Oh, it was a great noise that would frighten a monster's ear,
To make an earthquake! sure, it was the roar
Or make an earthquake! I'm sure it was the roar
Of a whole herd of lions.

Of a whole herd of lions.

ALONSO
Heard you this, Gonzalo?
Did you here this Gonzalo?

GONZALO
Upon mine honour, sir, I heard a humming,
On my honor, sir, I heard a humming,
And that a strange one too, which did awake me:
And it was a strange one too, that did awaken me:
I shaked you, sir, and cried: as mine eyes open'd,
I shook you, sir, and cried out: as my eyes opened
I saw their weapons drawn: there was a noise,
I saw their weapons drawn: there was a noise,
That's verily. 'Tis best we stand upon our guard,
It's true. It's best we stand on our guard,
Or that we quit this place; let's draw our weapons.
Or that we leave this place; let's draw our weapons.

ALONSO
Lead off this ground; and let's make further search
Lead away from this ground; and let's search further
For my poor son.
For my poor son.

GONZALO
Heavens keep him from these beasts!
Heavens keep him from these beasts!
For he is, sure, i' the island.
For he is surely on the island.

ALONSO
Lead away.
Lead the way.

ARIEL
Prospero my lord shall know what I have done:
Propsero, my lord will know what I have done:
So, king, go safely on to seek thy son.
So, king, go safely to search for your son.

Exeunt

SCENE II.

Another part of the island.
Enter CALIBAN with a burden of wood. A noise of thunder heard

CALIBAN
All the infections that the sun sucks up
All the diseases that the sun picks up
From bogs, fens, flats, on Prosper fall and make him
From bogs, marshes, swamps, on Prospero fall and make him
By inch-meal a disease! His spirits hear me
Inch by inch into a disease! His spirits hear me
And yet I needs must curse. But they'll nor pinch,
But still I need to curse him. But they won't pinch,
Fright me with urchin--shows, pitch me i' the mire,
Scare me with goblins, throw me in the mud,
Nor lead me, like a firebrand, in the dark
Or lead me, like a torch, into the dark
Out of my way, unless he bid 'em; but
Out of my way, unless he tell them to: but
For every trifle are they set upon me;
For every little thing they are set upon me;
Sometime like apes that mow and chatter at me
Sometimes like apes that grimace and chatter at me
And after bite me, then like hedgehogs which
And then bite me, and then like hedgehogs which
Lie tumbling in my barefoot way and mount
Like tumbling in the way of my bare get and jab
Their pricks at my footfall; sometime am I
Their pines at my foot steps; sometimes I am
All wound with adders who with cloven tongues
All wound up with snakes whose split tongues
Do hiss me into madness.
Hiss me into madness.

Enter TRINCULO

Lo, now, lo!
Look here, no!
Here comes a spirit of his, and to torment me
Here comes a spirit of his, and to torment me
For bringing wood in slowly. I'll fall flat;
For bring in the wood too slowly. I'll fall flat on the ground;
Perchance he will not mind me.
Perhaps he won't notice me.

TRINCULO
Here's neither bush nor shrub, to bear off
There's not a bush or a shrub to keep off
any weather at all, and another storm brewing;
Any weather at all, and another storm is brewing;
I hear it sing i' the wind: yond same black
I hear it singing in the wind: that very same black
cloud, yond huge one, looks like a foul
Cloud, that huge one, looks like a dreadful
bombard that would shed his liquor. If it
Wine-jug that would drop its liquid. If it
should thunder as it did before, I know not
Should thunder like it did before, I don't know
where to hide my head: yond same cloud cannot
Where to hide my head: that very same cloud cannot
choose but fall by pailfuls. What have we
Choose to fall in anything except buckets. What have we
here? a man or a fish? dead or alive? A fish:
Here? A man or a fish? Dead or alive? A fish:
he smells like a fish; a very ancient and fish-
He smells like a fish: a very ancient and fish-
like smell; a kind of not of the newest Poor-
Like smell; the kind from the less fresh dried
John. A strange fish! Were I in England now,
Fish. A strange fish! If I were in England now,
as once I was, and had but this fish painted,
As I once was, and had only this fish painted on a sign,
not a holiday fool there but would give a piece
Not a fool on vacation there who wouldn't give me a
of silver: there would this monster make a
Silver coin: there this monster would make a man a fortune;
man; any strange beast there makes a man:
Any strange beast there makes a man a fortune:
when they will not give a doit to relieve a lame
When they won't give a little coin to save a lame
beggar, they will lazy out ten to see a dead
Beggar, they will give out ten coins to see a dead
Indian. Legged like a man and his fins like
Indian. Legs like a man and his fins like
arms! Warm o' my troth! I do now let loose
Arms! He's actually warm! I now let go of
my opinion; hold it no longer: this is no fish,

My opinions; and hold it no longer: this isn't a fish
but an islander, that hath lately suffered by a
But an islander, who has recently collapsed form a
thunderbolt.
Thunderbolt.

Thunder

Alas, the storm is come again! my best way is to
Sadly, the storm is coming again! The best thing for me is to
creep under his gaberdine; there is no other
Crawl under his cloak; there is no other
shelter hereabouts: misery acquaints a man with
Shelter around here: misery meets with a man who has
strange bed-fellows. I will here shroud till the
Strange bedfellows. I will shelter here until the
dregs of the storm be past.
Worst of the storm has passed.

Enter STEPHANO, singing: a bottle in his hand

STEPHANO
I shall no more to sea, to sea,
I will go no more out to sea, out to sea,
Here shall I die ashore—
Here I will die on land--
This is a very scurvy tune to sing at a man's
This is a very wretched song to sing at a man's
funeral: well, here's my comfort.
Funeral: well, here's my consolation.

Drinks

Sings

The master, the swabber, the boatswain and I,
The master, the deckhand, the boatswain and I,
The gunner and his mate
The gunner and his friend
Loved Mall, Meg and Marian and Margery,
Loved Mall, Meg and Marian and Margery,
But none of us cared for Kate;
But none of us cared for Kate;
For she had a tongue with a tang,

Because she had a tongue with a sharp edge,
Would cry to a sailor, Go hang!
And would yell to a sailor, 'Go hang yourself!'
She loved not the savour of tar nor of pitch,
She didn't love the smell of tar or of pitch,
Yet a tailor might scratch her where'er she did itch:
But an unmanly tailor might scratch her where she itched:
Then to sea, boys, and let her go hang!
Then off to sea, boys, and let her go hang!
This is a scurvy tune too: but here's my comfort.
This is a wretched song too: but here's my consolation.

Drinks

CALIBAN
Do not torment me: Oh!
Stop tormenting me: oh!

STEPHANO
What's the matter? Have we devils here? Do you put
What's the matter? Do we have devils here? Do you cast
tricks upon's with savages and men of Ind, ha? I
Spells on us with savages and the men of India, ha? I
have not scaped drowning to be afeard now of your
Have not escaped drowning to be afraid now of your
four legs; for it hath been said, As proper a man as
Four legs; for it has been said, 'As good of a man that
ever went on four legs cannot make him give ground;
Ever went on four legs cannot make him give up ground';
and it shall be said so again while Stephano
And it will be said again while Stephano
breathes at's nostrils.
Breathes through his nostrils.

CALIBAN
The spirit torments me; Oh!
The spirit torments me: oh!

STEPHANO
This is some monster of the isle with four legs, who
This is some monster of the island with four legs, who
hath got, as I take it, an ague. Where the devil
Has got, as I think, a fever. How the devil
should he learn our language? I will give him some

Has he learned our language? I will give him some
relief, if it be but for that. if I can recover him
Relief, it only because of that. If I can heal him
and keep him tame and get to Naples with him, he's a
And keep him tame and get to Naples with him, he's a
present for any emperor that ever trod on neat's leather.
Present fit for any emperor that's ever walked on cow leather.

CALIBAN

Do not torment me, prithee; I'll bring my wood home faster.
Don't torment me, please: I'll bring the wood home faster.

STEPHANO

He's in his fit now and does not talk after the
He's in a fit of convulsions from the fever now and doesn't talk with
wisest. He shall taste of my bottle: if he have
Good sense. He'll take a drink form my bottle: if he has
never drunk wine afore will go near to remove his
Never drunk wine before it will nearly take away his
fit. If I can recover him and keep him tame, I will
Convulsions. If I can heal him and keep him tame, they won't
not take too much for him; he shall pay for him that
Be able to pay me enough for him; he will bring in enough money for the man
hath him, and that soundly.
That has him, and do it well.

CALIBAN

Thou dost me yet but little hurt; thou wilt anon, I
As of now you have done me little harm; but you will soon, I
know it by thy trembling: now Prosper works upon thee.
Can tell by your trembling: now Prospero is working his magic on you.

STEPHANO

Come on your ways; open your mouth; here is that
Come along; open your mouth; here is the drink
which will give language to you, cat: open your
That will make even you speak, cat: open your
mouth; this will shake your shaking, I can tell you,
Mouth; this will shake off your convulsions, I can tell you that,
and that soundly: you cannot tell who's your friend:
And it'll do it well: you cannot tell who's your friend:
open your chaps again.
Open you mouth again.

TRINCULO

I should know that voice: it should be--but he is
I know that voice: it is—but he's
drowned; and these are devils: O defend me!
Drowned; and these are devils: Oh, help me!

STEPHANO

Four legs and two voices: a most delicate monster!
Four legs and two voices: a most delightful monster!
His forward voice now is to speak well of his
His frontward voice is for speaking well of his
friend; his backward voice is to utter foul speeches
Friend; and his backward voice is for speaking terrible remarks
and to detract. If all the wine in my bottle will
And to criticize. If all the wine in my bottle will
recover him, I will help his ague. Come. Amen! I
Heal him, I will get rid of his fever. Come on. Amen! I
will pour some in thy other mouth.
Will pour some of this in your other mouth.

TRINCULO

Stephano!
Stephano!

STEPHANO

Doth thy other mouth call me? Mercy, mercy! This is
Does you other mouth call my name? Mercy, mercy! This is
a devil, and no monster: I will leave him; I have no
A devil, not a monster: I will leave him be; I don't have
long spoon.
A long spoon needed to feed a devil.

TRINCULO

Stephano! If thou beest Stephano, touch me and
Stephano! If you are Stephano, touch me and
speak to me: for I am Trinculo--be not afeard—thy
Speak to me: for I am Trinculo—don't be afraid—your
good friend Trinculo.
Good friend Trinculo.

STEPHANO

If thou beest Trinculo, come forth: I'll pull thee
If you are Trinculo, come out: I'll pull you
by the lesser legs: if any be Trinculo's legs,

By the smaller legs: if any are Trinculo's legs,
these are they. Thou art very Trinculo indeed! How
Those ones are. You are really Trinculo, indeed! How
camest thou to be the siege of this moon-calf? Can
Did you come to be the dung of this monster? Can
he vent Trinculos?
He excrete Trinculos?

TRINCULO
I took him to be killed with a thunder-stroke. But
I thought he has been killed by a thunderbolt. But
art thou not drowned, Stephano? I hope now thou art
How are you not drowned, Stephano? Now, I hope you're
not drowned. Is the storm overblown? I hid me
Not drowned. Has the storm blown away? I hid myself
under the dead moon-calf's gaberdine for fear of
Under the dead monster's cloak from fear of
the storm. And art thou living, Stephano? O
The strom. And are you alive, Stephano? Oh,
Stephano, two Neapolitans 'scaped!
Stephano, two of us men from Naples escaped!

STEPHANO
Prithee, do not turn me about; my stomach is not constant.
Please, don't dance around with me; my stomach isn't steady.

CALIBAN
[Aside] These be fine things, an if they be
[Aside] These are fine creatures, if they aren't
not sprites.
Spirits.
That's a brave god and bears celestial liquor.
That's a brave god and he carried godly wine.
I will kneel to him.
I will kneel to him.

STEPHANO
How didst thou 'scape? How camest thou hither?
How did you escape? How did you come to be here?
swear by this bottle how thou camest hither. I
Swear to me by this bottle how you came to be here. I
escaped upon a butt of sack which the sailors
Escaped on a barrel of wine that the sailors
heaved o'erboard, by this bottle; which I made of

Threw overboard, I swear by this bottle; which I made out of
the bark of a tree with mine own hands since I was
Tree bark with my own hands when I was
cast ashore.
Cast on shore.

CALIBAN
I'll swear upon that bottle to be thy true subject;
I'll sear on that bottle to be your worshiper;
for the liquor is not earthly.
Because that wine is not of this world.

STEPHANO
Here; swear then how thou escapedst.
Here then; tell me how you escaped.

TRINCULO
Swum ashore. man, like a duck: I can swim like a
I swam ashore, man, like a duck: I can swim like a
duck, I'll be sworn.
Duck, I'll swear that.

STEPHANO
Here, kiss the book. Though thou canst swim like a
Swear on the holy book. Though you can swim like a
duck, thou art made like a goose.
Duck, you are built like a goose.

TRINCULO
O Stephano. hast any more of this?
Oh, Stephano, do you have any more of this?

STEPHANO
The whole butt, man: my cellar is in a rock by the
The whole barrel, man: my makeshift wine-cellar is in a rock
sea-side where my wine is hid. How now, moon-calf!
By the sea-side where I hid my wine. What about you, monster!
how does thine ague?
How is your fever?

CALIBAN
Hast thou not dropp'd from heaven?
Have you not fallen form heaven?

STEPHANO

Out o' the moon, I do assure thee: I was the man i'
From the moon, I promise you: I was the man in
the moon when time was.
The moon, once upon a time.

CALIBAN

I have seen thee in her and I do adore thee:
I have seen you in the moon and I love you:
My mistress show'd me thee and thy dog and thy bush.
My mistress showed you to me, and your little dog and your thornbush.

STEPHANO

Come, swear to that; kiss the book: I will furnish
Come on, swear to that; swear on the holy book: I will supply
it anon with new contents swear.
More soon with new wine, I sear.

TRINCULO

By this good light, this is a very shallow monster!
By heavens, this is a very gullible monster!
I afeard of him! A very weak monster! The man i'
I was scared of him! A very weak monster! The man in
the moon! A most poor credulous monster! Well
The moon! A very gullible monster! Well
drawn, monster, in good sooth!
Drink deep, monster, in good health!

CALIBAN

I'll show thee every fertile inch o' th' island;
I'll show you every fertile inch of the island;
And I will kiss thy foot: I prithee, be my god.
And I will kiss your feet: please, be my god.

TRINCULO

By this light, a most perfidious and drunken
By heavens, a very treacherous and drunken
monster! when 's god's asleep, he'll rob his bottle.
Monster! When his god is asleep, he'll steal his wine.

CALIBAN

I'll kiss thy foot; I'll swear myself thy subject.
I'll kiss your feet; I'll swear to be your worshiper.

STEPHANO

Come on then; down, and swear.
Come on then; kneel down, and swear.

TRINCULO

I shall laugh myself to death at this puppy-headed
I will laugh myself to death at this puppy-headed
monster. A most scurvy monster! I could find in my
Monster. A most wretched monster! If I could find it in my
heart to beat him,--
Heart to beat him,--

STEPHANO

Come, kiss.
Come on, kiss my feet.

TRINCULO

But that the poor monster's in drink: an abominable monster!
Except that the poor monster is drunk: a despicable monster!

CALIBAN

I'll show thee the best springs; I'll pluck thee berries;
I'll show you the best spring; I'll pick you berries;
I'll fish for thee and get thee wood enough.
I'll fish for you and get you enough wood.
A plague upon the tyrant that I serve!
May a plague infect the tyrant that I serve!
I'll bear him no more sticks, but follow thee,
I'll carry no more sticks for him, but instead follow you,
Thou wondrous man.
You wonderful man.

TRINCULO

A most ridiculous monster, to make a wonder of a
A most ridiculous monster, to think that a poor drunkard
Poor drunkard!
Is wonderful!

CALIBAN

I prithee, let me bring thee where crabs grow;
Please, let me take you to where the crab-apples grow;
And I with my long nails will dig thee pignuts;

And with my long fingernails I will dig up edible roots for you;
Show thee a jay's nest and instruct thee how
Show you the jay-bird's nest and instruct you on how
To snare the nimble marmoset; I'll bring thee
To catch the nimble marmoset; I'll take you
To clustering filberts and sometimes I'll get thee
To the clustering hazelnuts and sometimes I'll get you
Young scamels from the rock. Wilt thou go with me?
Young clams from the rock. Will you come with me?

STEPHANO
I prithee now, lead the way without any more
Please, lead the way without any more
talking. Trinculo, the king and all our company
Talking. Trinculo, the king and all our other companions
else being drowned, we will inherit here: here;
Having been drowned, we will rule here: here;
bear my bottle: fellow Trinculo, we'll fill him by
Carry my bottle: my friend Trinculo, we'll fill it
and by again.
Soon enough.

CALIBAN
[Sings drunkenly]
[Sings drunkenly]
Farewell master; farewell, farewell!
Good bye my old master; good bye, good bye!

TRINCULO
A howling monster: a drunken monster!
A screaming monster: a drunken monster!

CALIBAN
No more dams I'll make for fish
I'll make no more dams to catch fish,
Nor fetch in firing
Nor bring in the firewood
At requiring;
At your demand;
Nor scrape trencher, nor wash dish
Nor scrape off your plate, nor wash your dishes,
'Ban, 'Ban, Cacaliban
'Ban, 'Ban, Cacaliban
Has a new master: get a new man.

Has a new master: get a new slave.
Freedom, hey-day! hey-day, freedom! freedom,
Freedom, hey-day! Hey-day, freedom! Freedom,
hey-day, freedom!
Hey-day, freedom!

STEPHANO
O brave monster! Lead the way.
Oh splendid monster! Lead the way.

Exeunt

ACT III

SCENE I.

Before PROSPERO'S Cell.
Enter FERDINAND, bearing a log

FERDINAND
There be some sports are painful, and their labour
There are some sports that are difficult, and their difficulty
Delight in them sets off: some kinds of baseness
Is what makes them delightful: some kinds of shameful activities
Are nobly undergone and most poor matters
Are undertaken honorably and most poor activists
Point to rich ends. This my mean task
Are directed to rich ends. My lowly task here
Would be as heavy to me as odious, but
Would be as difficult to me as it is repulsive, except
The mistress which I serve quickens what's dead
That the mistress whom I serve gives life to the dead
And makes my labours pleasures: O, she is
And makes my forced-work pleasurable: oh, she is
Ten times more gentle than her father's crabbed,
Then times more gentle than her father is bad-tempered,
And he's composed of harshness. I must remove
And he's made up of harshness. I must remove
Some thousands of these logs and pile them up,
Several thousands of these logs and pile them up,
Upon a sore injunction: my sweet mistress
Under a hard order: my sweet mistress
Weeps when she sees me work, and says, such baseness
Weeps when she sees me work, and says, such lowly work
Had never like executor. I forget:
Has never been done by someone like me. I forget my work:
But these sweet thoughts do even refresh my labours,
But even these sweet thoughts revitalize my tasks,
Most busy lest, when I do it.
So that when I am busy at work I am not really doing it but instead thinking of those thoughts.

Enter MIRANDA; and PROSPERO at a distance, unseen

MIRANDA

Alas, now, pray you,
Sadly, now, please,
Work not so hard: I would the lightning had
Don't work so hard: I wish the lightning had
Burnt up those logs that you are enjoin'd to pile!
Burnt up those logs that you are ordered to pile!
Pray, set it down and rest you: when this burns,
Please, set it down and rest a bit: when this wood burns,
'Twill weep for having wearied you. My father
It will weep for having tired you out. My father
Is hard at study; pray now, rest yourself;
Is studying hard; please, rest yourself a bit;
He's safe for these three hours.
He's safely out of the way for three hours.

FERDINAND

O most dear mistress,
Oh, dearest mistress,
The sun will set before I shall discharge
The sun will set before I will finish
What I must strive to do.
What I must try to do.

MIRANDA

If you'll sit down,
If you'll sit down,
I'll bear your logs the while: pray, give me that;
I'll carry your logs for a while: please, give me that;
I'll carry it to the pile.
I'll bring it to the pile.

FERDINAND

No, precious creature;
No, precious lady;
I had rather crack my sinews, break my back,
I would rather tear my muscles, and break my back,
Than you should such dishonour undergo,
Than have you take up such shameful labor
While I sit lazy by.
While I sit here lazily.

MIRANDA

It would become me

It would be as fitting for me
As well as it does you: and I should do it
As it is for you: and I would do it
With much more ease; for my good will is to it,
Much more easily; because my good will behind it,
And yours it is against.
And yours is against it.

PROSPERO
Poor worm, thou art infected!
Little girl, you are infected with love!
This visitation shows it.
This visit shows it.

MIRANDA
You look wearily.
You look tired.

FERDINAND
No, noble mistress;'tis fresh morning with me
No, noble mistress; it's still a fresh morning for me
When you are by at night. I do beseech you—
When you have been by all night. I do ask you—
Chiefly that I might set it in my prayers—
Mostly so that I can place it in my prayers—
What is your name?
What is your name?

MIRANDA
Miranda.--O my father,
Miranda.—Oh, my father,
I have broke your hest to say so!
I have broken your command by saying that!

FERDINAND
Admired Miranda!
Admired Miranda!
Indeed the top of admiration! Worth
Indeed the peak of amazement! Worth
What's dearest to the world! Full many a lady
Whatever is most valuable in all the world! A good many women
I have eyed with best regard and many a time
I have looked at with a high regard and many times
The harmony of their tongues hath into bondage

The sound of their voices has captured
Brought my too diligent ear: for several virtues
My overly attentive ear: for several virtues
Have I liked several women; never any
Have I liked several women; never any
With so fun soul, but some defect in her
With such a good soul, but some defect in her
Did quarrel with the noblest grace she owed
Did argue with the most noble grace she possessed
And put it to the foil: but you, O you,
And defeated it: but you, oh you,
So perfect and so peerless, are created
So perfect and so peerless, are created
Of every creature's best!
Better than everyone else!

MIRANDA
I do not know
I don't know
One of my sex; no woman's face remember,
Another woman; I remember no woman's face,
Save, from my glass, mine own; nor have I seen
Except, from the mirror, my own; nor have I seen
More that I may call men than you, good friend,
More people that I can call men than you, good friend,
And my dear father: how features are abroad,
And my dear father: what people look like elsewhere in the world,
I am skilless of; but, by my modesty,
I am unaware of; but, by my virtue,
The jewel in my dower, I would not wish
And the jewels in my dowry, I wouldn't want
Any companion in the world but you,
Any companion in the world but you,
Nor can imagination form a shape,
Nor can I imagine any figure
Besides yourself, to like of. But I prattle
Besides yourself, to like. But I am babbling
Something too wildly and my father's precepts
Somewhat too wildly and my father's instructions
I therein do forget.
I am forgetting.

FERDINAND
I am in my condition

I am ranked as
A prince, Miranda; I do think, a king;
A prince, Miranda; and I do believe, as a king;
I would, not so!--and would no more endure
I wish it were not so!—and would no more endure
This wooden slavery than to suffer
This inferior slavery than I would allow
The flesh-fly blow my mouth. Hear my soul speak:
A fly lay eggs in my mouth. Listen to my soul speak:
The very instant that I saw you, did
The very moment that I saw you,
My heart fly to your service; there resides,
My heart flew to your service; there it stays,
To make me slave to it; and for your sake
Making me a slave to you; and for your sake
Am I this patient log--man.
I am this patient log-carrier.

MIRANDA
Do you love me?
Do you love me?

FERDINAND
O heaven, O earth, bear witness to this sound
Oh heaven, oh earth, be the witness to what I will say,
And crown what I profess with kind event
And top off what I say with a happy outcome
If I speak true! if hollowly, invert
If what is say is true! If it is false, switch
What best is boded me to mischief! I
what good is destined for me to misfortune! I
Beyond all limit of what else i' the world
Beyond the limit of everything else in the world,
Do love, prize, honour you.
Do love, prize and honor you.

MIRANDA
I am a fool
I am a fool
To weep at what I am glad of.
To weep at what I am glad to hear.

PROSPERO
Fair encounter

What a wonderful meeting
Of two most rare affections! Heavens rain grace
Between two splendid loves! Heavens rain down virtue
On that which breeds between 'em!
On that which develops between them!

FERDINAND
Wherefore weep you?
Why do you weep?

MIRANDA
At mine unworthiness that dare not offer
At my unworthiness that doesn't dare to offer
What I desire to give, and much less take
What I want to give you, and dares much less to take
What I shall die to want. But this is trifling;
What I will die from wanting so much. But this is foolish;
And all the more it seeks to hide itself,
And the more it tries to hide itself,
The bigger bulk it shows. Hence, bashful cunning!
The more it shows. So this reserved craftiness!
And prompt me, plain and holy innocence!
And help me, plain and holy innocence!
I am your wife, if you will marry me;
I am your wife, if you will marry me;
If not, I'll die your maid: to be your fellow
If not, I'll die as your maid: to be your wife
You may deny me; but I'll be your servant,
You can deny me; but I'll be your servant,
Whether you will or no.
Whether you like it or no.

FERDINAND
My mistress, dearest;
My mistress, dearest;
And I thus humble ever.
And I will be that lowly as well for ever.

MIRANDA
My husband, then?
You will be my husband then?

FERDINAND
Ay, with a heart as willing

Yes, with as heart as willing
As bondage e'er of freedom: here's my hand.
As oppression is willing of freedom: here's my hand.

MIRANDA
And mine, with my heart in't; and now farewell
And mine, with my heart in it; and now good bye
Till half an hour hence.
Till half an hour from now.

FERDINAND
A thousand thousand!
A million good byes!

Exeunt FERDINAND and MIRANDA severally

PROSPERO
So glad of this as they I cannot be,
I cannot be as happy about this as they are,
Who are surprised withal; but my rejoicing
Who are surprised by everything; but my rejoicing
At nothing can be more. I'll to my book,
At nothing can be more. I'll go to my cooks
For yet ere supper-time must I perform
For still before supper-time I must perform
Much business appertaining.
Many related tasks.

Exit

SCENE II.
Another part of the island.
Enter CALIBAN, STEPHANO, and TRINCULO

STEPHANO
Tell not me; when the butt is out, we will drink
Don't tell me; when the barrel is out, we'll drink
water; not a drop before: therefore bear up, and
Water; not a drop before: so don't fall over, and
board 'em. Servant-monster, drink to me.
Get on board. Servant-monster, drink to me

TRINCULO
Servant-monster! the folly of this island! They

Servant-monster! The silliness of this island! They
say there's but five upon this isle: we are three
Say there's only five people on this island: we are three
of them; if th' other two be brained like us, the
Of them; if the other two are addle-brained like us, the
state totters.
Government will fall.

STEPHANO
Drink, servant-monster, when I bid thee: thy eyes
Drink, servant-monster, when I tell you to: your eyes
are almost set in thy head.
Are almost fixed in your head.

TRINCULO
Where should they be set else? he were a brave
Where else should they be? He would an excellent
monster indeed, if they were set in his tail.
Monster indeed, if his eyes where fixed on his tail.

STEPHANO
My man-monster hath drown'd his tongue in sack:
My man-monster has drowned his tongue in wine:
for my part, the sea cannot drown me; I swam, ere I
For me, even the sea cannot drown me; I swam, before I
could recover the shore, five and thirty leagues off
Could reach the shore, some thirty-five leagues off
and on. By this light, thou shalt be my lieutenant,
And on. By heaven, you shall be my lieutenant,
monster, or my standard.
Monster, or my flagbearer.

TRINCULO
Your lieutenant, if you list; he's no standard.
Your lieutenant, if you want; he's no flagbearer.

STEPHANO
We'll not run, Monsieur Monster.
We won't run from battle, Mister Monster.

TRINCULO
Nor go neither; but you'll lie like dogs and yet say
Or go to battle either; but you'll lie like dogs and still say
nothing neither.

Nothing at the same time.

STEPHANO
Moon-calf, speak once in thy life, if thou beest a
Monster, speak once in your life, if you are a
good moon-calf.
Good monster.

CALIBAN
How does thy honour? Let me lick thy shoe.
How are you, my honor? Let me lick you shoe.
I'll not serve him; he's not valiant.
I won't serve him; he's not valiant.

TRINCULO
Thou liest, most ignorant monster: I am in case to
You lie, you very dim-witted monster: I am in condition to
justle a constable. Why, thou deboshed fish thou,
Fight a police officer. Why, you depraved fish you,
was there ever man a coward that hath drunk so much
Was there ever a cowardly man who has drunk as much
sack as I to-day? Wilt thou tell a monstrous lie,
Wine as I have today? Will you tell a monstrous lie,
being but half a fish and half a monster?
Since you are only half fish and half monster?

CALIBAN
Lo, how he mocks me! wilt thou let him, my lord?
Look, how me makes fun of me! Will you let him, my lord?

TRINCULO
'Lord' quoth he! That a monster should be such a natural!
'Lord', he calls you! How could a monster be such an idiot!

CALIBAN
Lo, lo, again! bite him to death, I prithee.
Look, again! Bite him to death, please.

STEPHANO
Trinculo, keep a good tongue in your head: if you
Trinculo, speak politely: if you
prove a mutineer,--the next tree! The poor monster's
Try and mutiny,--I'll hang you from the next tree! The poor monster is
my subject and he shall not suffer indignity.

My subject and he will not suffer humiliation.

CALIBAN
I thank my noble lord. Wilt thou be pleased to
Thank you my noble lord. Would you like to
hearken once again to the suit I made to thee?
Listen again to the request I made you?

STEPHANO
Marry, will I kneel and repeat it; I will stand,
By the Holy Virgin, I will. Kneel down and repeat it; I will stand,
and so shall Trinculo.
And so will Trinculo.

Enter ARIEL, invisible

CALIBAN
As I told thee before, I am subject to a tyrant, a
As I told you before, I am the servant to a tyrant, a
sorcerer, that by his cunning hath cheated me of the island.
Sorcerer, that by his trickery has cheated me out of the island.

ARIEL
Thou liest.
You lie.

CALIBAN
Thou liest, thou jesting monkey, thou: I would my
You like, you joking monkey you: I would like for my
valiant master would destroy thee! I do not lie.
Virtuous master to destroy you! I do not lie.

STEPHANO
Trinculo, if you trouble him any more in's tale, by
Trinculo, if you interrupt him again in his story, with
this hand, I will supplant some of your teeth.
This hand, I will knock out your teeth.

TRINCULO
Why, I said nothing.
But, I didn't say anything.

STEPHANO
Mum, then, and no more. Proceed.

Silent, then, and don't speak again. Continue.

CALIBAN
I say, by sorcery he got this isle;
I tell you, it was by sorcery that he got this island;
From me he got it. if thy greatness will
He got it from me. If your greatness will
Revenge it on him,--for I know thou darest,
Take revenge on him for it,--because I know you are brave enough,
But this thing dare not,--
But this other man is not,--

STEPHANO
That's most certain.
That's most certain.

CALIBAN
Thou shalt be lord of it and I'll serve thee.
You will be lord of the island, and I'll serve you.

STEPHANO
How now shall this be compassed?
Now, how will this be accomplished?
Canst thou bring me to the party?
Con you bring me to this man?

CALIBAN
Yea, yea, my lord: I'll yield him thee asleep,
Yes, yes, my lord: I'll bring him to you asleep,
Where thou mayst knock a nail into his bead.
So you can knock a nail into his head.

ARIEL
Thou liest; thou canst not.
You lie; you can't do that.

CALIBAN
What a pied ninny's this! Thou scurvy patch!
What a patched up fool he is! You wretched fool!
I do beseech thy greatness, give him blows
I beg your greatness, hit him
And take his bottle from him: when that's gone
And take his bottle from him: when that's gone
He shall drink nought but brine; for I'll not show him

He will drink nothing but sea-water; because I won't show him
Where the quick freshes are.
Where the fresh water is.

STEPHANO
Trinculo, run into no further danger:
Trinculo, don't put yourself danger:
interrupt the monster one word further, and,
If you interrupt the monster again, then
by this hand, I'll turn my mercy out o' doors
By this hand, I'll have no mercy
and make a stock-fish of thee.
And turn you into a dried fish.

TRINCULO
Why, what did I? I did nothing. I'll go farther
Why, what did I do? I did nothing. I move farther
off.
Away.

STEPHANO
Didst thou not say he lied?
Didn't you say that he lied?

ARIEL
Thou liest.
You lie.

STEPHANO
Do I so? take thou that.
Do I? take that.

Beats TRINCULO

As you like this, give me the lie another time.
If you like this, tell me that I'm lying again.

TRINCULO
I did not give the lie. Out o' your
I didn't day that you lied. Are you out of your
wits and bearing too? A pox o' your bottle!
Mind and deaf as well? Curse your bottle!
this can sack and drinking do. A murrain on

This is what wine and drinking do. Curse
your monster, and the devil take your fingers!
Your monster, and may the devil take your fingers!

CALIBAN
Ha, ha, ha!
Ha, ha, ha!

STEPHANO
Now, forward with your tale. Prithee, stand farther
Now, continue with your tale. Please, stand farther
off.
Away.

CALIBAN
Beat him enough: after a little time
If you beat him enough: after a little while
I'll beat him too.
I'll beat him too.

STEPHANO
Stand farther. Come, proceed.
Stand farther away. Come on, continue.

CALIBAN
Why, as I told thee, 'tis a custom with him,
Why, as I told you, he has a habit
I' th' afternoon to sleep: there thou mayst brain him,
Of sleeping in the afternoon: you can bash his head in then,
Having first seized his books, or with a log
After you have taken his books, or with a log
Batter his skull, or paunch him with a stake,
You could smash his skull, or stab him in the stomach with a stake,
Or cut his wezand with thy knife. Remember
Or cut his throat with your knife. Remember
First to possess his books; for without them
First to take his books; because without them
He's but a sot, as I am, nor hath not
He's just an idiot like I am, and he won't have
One spirit to command: they all do hate him
One spirit to command: they all hate him
As rootedly as I. Burn but his books.
As deep-seatedly as I do. Burn only his books.
He has brave utensils,--for so he calls them—

He has fine tools,--that is what he calls them--
Which when he has a house, he'll deck withal
Which he'll decorate his house with, when he has one.
And that most deeply to consider is
And the thing to thing about most deeply is
The beauty of his daughter; he himself
The beauty of his daughter; he himself
Calls her a nonpareil: I never saw a woman,
Call her a woman without equal: I've never seen another woman
But only Sycorax my dam and she;
Besides my mother Sycorax and her;
But she as far surpasseth Sycorax
But she surpasses Sycroax as far
As great'st does least.
As the greatest surpasses the lowest.

STEPHANO
Is it so brave a lass?
Is she so excellent a girl?

CALIBAN
Ay, lord; she will become thy bed, I warrant.
Yes, lord; she will grace your bed, I promise.
And bring thee forth brave brood.
And give you excellent children.

STEPHANO
Monster, I will kill this man: his daughter and I
Monster, I will kill this man: his daughter and I
will be king and queen--save our graces!—and
Will be king and queen—God save our royalty!--and
Trinculo and thyself shall be viceroys. Dost thou
Trinculo and yourself will be deputy monarchs. Do you
like the plot, Trinculo?
Like the plan, Trinculo?

TRINCULO
Excellent.
It's an excellent plan.

STEPHANO
Give me thy hand: I am sorry I beat thee; but,
Give me your hand: I am sorry I beat you; but,
while thou livest, keep a good tongue in thy head.

While you live, you must be polite.

CALIBAN
Within this half hour will he be asleep:
Within half-an-hour he will be asleep:
Wilt thou destroy him then?
Will you destroy him then?

STEPHANO
Ay, on mine honour.
Yes, I swear on my honor.

ARIEL
This will I tell my master.
I will tell my master about this.

CALIBAN
Thou makest me merry; I am full of pleasure:
You make me happy; I am full of joy:
Let us be jocund: will you troll the catch
Let us be joyful: will you sing the musical round
You taught me but while-ere?
You taught me only a while ago?

STEPHANO
At thy request, monster, I will do reason, any
At your request, monster, I will do what is reasonable, anything
reason. Come on, Trinculo, let us sing.
Reasonable. Come on, Trinculo, let's sing.

Sings

Flout 'em and scout 'em
Insult them and ridicule them
And scout 'em and flout 'em
And ridicule them and insult them
Thought is free.
Thought is free.

CALIBAN
That's not the tune.
That's not the song.

Ariel plays the tune on a tabour and pipe

"[Ariel plays the song on a small drum and a pipe]"

STEPHANO
What is this same?
What is this song?

TRINCULO
This is the tune of our catch, played by the picture
This is the tune of our musical round, played by the image
of Nobody.
Of no one at all.

STEPHANO
If thou beest a man, show thyself in thy likeness:
If you are a man, show yourself as you are:
if thou beest a devil, take't as thou list.
If you are a devil, take any form you would like.

TRINCULO
O, forgive me my sins!
Oh, forgive me for my sins!

STEPHANO
He that dies pays all debts: I defy thee. Mercy upon us!
A man that dies must pay all his debts: I will resist you. Show us mercy!

CALIBAN
Art thou afeard?
Are you afraid?

STEPHANO
No, monster, not I.
No, monster, I'm not.

CALIBAN
Be not afeard; the isle is full of noises,
Don't be afraid; the island is full of noises,
Sounds and sweet airs, that give delight and hurt not.
Sounds and sweet melodies, that give delight and don't hurt.
Sometimes a thousand twangling instruments
Sometimes a thousand jingling instruments
Will hum about mine ears, and sometime voices
Will hum around my ears, and sometimes voices
That, if I then had waked after long sleep,

That, even if I had just awaken from a long sleep,
Will make me sleep again: and then, in dreaming,
Would make me go to sleep again: and then, in my dreams,
The clouds methought would open and show riches
I would see clouds that I thought would open and show riches
Ready to drop upon me that, when I waked,
That were ready to fall down to me so that, when I awoke,
I cried to dream again.
I cried because I wanted to be dreaming again.

STEPHANO
This will prove a brave kingdom to me, where I shall
This will prove to be an excellent kingdom for me, where I will
have my music for nothing.
Have my music from thin air.

CALIBAN
When Prospero is destroyed.
When Prospero is destroyed.

STEPHANO
That shall be by and by: I remember the story.
That will happen immediately: I remember your story.

TRINCULO
The sound is going away; let's follow it, and
The sound is going away; let's follow it, and
after do our work.
Afterward do our work.

STEPHANO
Lead, monster; we'll follow. I would I could see
Lead the way, monster; we'll follow. I wish I could see
this tabourer; he lays it on.
This dummer; he plays energetically.

TRINCULO
Wilt come? I'll follow, Stephano.
Will you come on? I'll follow you, Stephano.

Exeunt

SCENE III.
Another part of the island.

Enter ALONSO, SEBASTIAN, ANTONIO, GONZALO, ADRIAN, FRANCISCO, and others

GONZALO
By'r lakin, I can go no further, sir;
By our Lady Mary, I can't go any further, sir;
My old bones ache: here's a maze trod indeed
My old bones ache: we've walked a maze indeed
Through forth-rights and meanders! By your patience,
With straight and winding paths! Please be patient,
I needs must rest me.
I need to rest.

ALONSO
Old lord, I cannot blame thee,
Old lord, I cannot blame you,
Who am myself attach'd with weariness,
When I, myself, am also gripped by weariness
To the dulling of my spirits: sit down, and rest.
That is bringing down my spirits: sit down, and rest.
Even here I will put off my hope and keep it
Now I will have to let go off my hope and hold on to it
No longer for my flatterer: he is drown'd
No longer for the sake of he who tell me that my son isn't dead: he is drowned,
Whom thus we stray to find, and the sea mocks
The one who we are now wandering in order to find, and the sea makes fun
Our frustrate search on land. Well, let him go.
Of our frustrating search on land. Well, let him go.

ANTONIO
[Aside to SEBASTIAN] I am right glad that he's so
[Aside to SEBASTIAN] I'm really glad that he's so
out of hope.
Out of hope.
Do not, for one repulse, forego the purpose
Do not, because of one rebuff, give up on the plan
That you resolved to effect.
That you determined yourself to accomplish.

SEBASTIAN
[Aside to ANTONIO] The next advantage
[Aside to ANTONIO] We will thoroughly take
Will we take throughly.
The next opportunity.

ANTONIO

[Aside to SEBASTIAN] Let it be to-night;
[Aside to SEBASTIAN] Let's do it tonight;
For, now they are oppress'd with travel, they
Because, no they are wearied from walking, they
Will not, nor cannot, use such vigilance
Will not be able to, nor can they, use the same watchfulness
As when they are fresh.
As when they are fresh.

SEBASTIAN

[Aside to ANTONIO] I say, to-night: no more.
[Aside to ANTONIO] I say, tonight: let's speak no more.

Solemn and strange music

ALONSO

What harmony is this? My good friends, hark!
What music is this? My good friends, listen!

GONZALO

Marvellous sweet music!
Marvelous sweet music!

Enter PROSPERO above, invisible. Enter several strange Shapes, bringing in a banquet; they dance about it with gentle actions of salutation; and, inviting the King, & c. to eat, they depart

"[Enter PROSPERO above them and invisible. Enter several strange Ghostly Shapes, bring in a feast; they dance around it with kind welcoming guestures; and after they invite the King and his men to eat, they leave]"

ALONSO

Give us kind keepers, heavens! What were these?
You've given us kind guardian-angels, heaven! What were they?

SEBASTIAN

A living drollery. Now I will believe
A real-life puppet-show. Now I will believe
That there are unicorns, that in Arabia
That unicorns exist, and that in Arabia
There is one tree, the phoenix' throne, one phoenix
There is a tree that is the phoenix's throne, with a phoenix
At this hour reigning there.
Ruling from there even now.

ANTONIO
I'll believe both;
I'll believe in both;
And what does else want credit, come to me,
And whatever other mythical creatures want acknowledgment, come to me,
And I'll be sworn 'tis true: travellers ne'er did
And I'll swear you are real: travelers never did
lie,
Lie,
Though fools at home condemn 'em.
Although the fools at home don't believe them.

GONZALO
If in Naples
If in Naples
I should report this now, would they believe me?
I told this story now, would they believe me?
If I should say, I saw such islanders—
If I should say that I saw such islanders—
For, certes, these are people of the island—
For certainly, these are people of the island—
Who, though they are of monstrous shape, yet, note,
Who, though they look like monsters, still, notice
Their manners are more gentle-kind than of
That their manners are more gentle and more kind than many
Our human generation you shall find
You would find in our human family,
Many, nay, almost any.
Really, more than almost anyone.

PROSPERO
[Aside] Honest lord,
[Aside] Honestly, lord,
Thou hast said well; for some of you there present
You have said the truth; for some of you there now
Are worse than devils.
Are worse than devils.

ALONSO
I cannot too much muse
I can't marvel too much at
Such shapes, such gesture and such sound, expressing,

These shapes, and their gestures and their sound,
Although they want the use of tongue, a kind
Although they don't use words, they are expressing a sort
Of excellent dumb discourse.
Of excellent silent dialogue.

PROSPERO
[Aside] Praise in departing.
[Aside] Give praise only after everything is done.

FRANCISCO
They vanish'd strangely.
They disappeared surprisingly.

SEBASTIAN
No matter, since
It's no matter, since
They have left their viands behind; for we have stomachs.
They have left their food behind; and we have stomachs to fill.
Will't please you taste of what is here?
Would you like to taste what is here?

ALONSO
Not I.
I don't.

GONZALO
Faith, sir, you need not fear. When we were boys,
By heaven, sir, you don't need to be afraid. When we were boys,
Who would believe that there were mountaineers
Who would have believed that there were mountain-men
Dew-lapp'd like bulls, whose throats had hanging at 'em
With loose skin around their necks like bulls, whose throats had hanging around them
Wallets of flesh? or that there were such men
Bulging flesh? Or that there were some men
Whose heads stood in their breasts? which now we find
Whose heads came out of their chests? Now we'll find
Each putter-out of five for one will bring us
That each speculator gives five-to-one odds that a traveler will return
Good warrant of.
With promises that they're real.

ALONSO
I will stand to and feed,

I'll go forward and eat,
Although my last: no matter, since I feel
Although it may be my last: It's not matter, since I feel like
The best is past. Brother, my lord the duke,
The best of my life has passed. Brother, my lord the duke,
Stand to and do as we.
Come forward and eat as we are.

Thunder and lightning. Enter ARIEL, like a harpy; claps his wings upon the table; and, with a quaint device, the banquet vanishes

"[Thunder and lightning. Enter ARIEL, shaped like a harpy (a vulture with the head and chest of a woman); he slaps his wings on the table; and, strangely, the feast vanishes.]"

ARIEL
You are three men of sin, whom Destiny,
You three—Alonso, Antonio, and Sebastian—are men of sin, whom Destiny—
That hath to instrument this lower world
Which has it's control over this lower world
And what is in't, the never-surfeited sea
And everything that is in it— has forced the never-overflowing sea
Hath caused to belch up you; and on this island
To spit you out; and put you on this island
Where man doth not inhabit; you 'mongst men
That is not inhabited by men; you out of all men
Being most unfit to live. I have made you mad;
Are most unworthy to live. I have made you insane;
And even with such-like valour, men hang and drown
And even with your same courage, mad men may hang themselves and drown
Their proper selves.
Their very own lives.

ALONSO, SEBASTIAN & c. draw their swords

You fools! I and my fellows
You fools! I and my fellow spirits
Are ministers of Fate: the elements,
Are the officials of Fate: the material
Of whom your swords are temper'd, may as well
That your swords are made of, could as easily
Wound the loud winds, or with bemock'd-at stabs
Wound the roaring winds, or with futile stabs
Kill the still-closing waters, as diminish

Kill the continuously flowing waters, as you could harm
One dowle that's in my plume: my fellow-ministers
One feather that's in my tail: my fellow spirits
Are like invulnerable. If you could hurt,
Are similarly invincible. If you could hurt us,
Your swords are now too massy for your strengths
You swords would be to heavy for you streght
And will not be uplifted. But remember—
And you wouldn't be able to life them. But remember—
For that's my business to you--that you three
For that's what I'm here to tell you—that you three
From Milan did supplant good Prospero;
Took Milan over from the good Prospero;
Exposed unto the sea, which hath requit it,
Sent out into the sea—which it has rewarded you for—
Him and his innocent child: for which foul deed
Both him and his innocent child: for which evil act
The powers, delaying, not forgetting, have
The gods, while they delayed, did not forget, and have
Incensed the seas and shores, yea, all the creatures,
Urged the seas and the shores, yes, all the creatures,
Against your peace. Thee of thy son, Alonso,
To prevent your happiness. Your son, Alonso,
They have bereft; and do pronounce by me:
They have taken from you; and have ordered me:
Lingering perdition, worse than any death
To give you a slow destruction, worse than any death
Can be at once, shall step by step attend
That happens fast, I will step by step follow
You and your ways; whose wraths to guard you from—
You and your ways; to protect you from the wraths of these powers—
Which here, in this most desolate isle, else falls
Who here, on this most remote island, will otherwise fall
Upon your heads--is nothing but heart-sorrow
On you heads—the only thing you can do is regret
And a clear life ensuing.
And lead a better life afterwards

He vanishes in thunder; then, to soft music enter the Shapes again, and dance, with mocks and mows, and carrying out the table

"[He vanishes in thunder; then to soft music the Ghostly Shapes enter again, and dance, with scornful gestures and grimaces, and carry away the table.]"

PROSPERO
Bravely the figure of this harpy hast thou
You have excellently performed the role of this harpy,
Perform'd, my Ariel; a grace it had, devouring:
My Ariel; it had a certain elegance as it made the food disappear:
Of my instruction hast thou nothing bated
You have left out nothing from my instructions
In what thou hadst to say: so, with good life
About what you had to say: and with good spirits
And observation strange, my meaner ministers
And special attention, so too have my lower-ranked spirits
Their several kinds have done. My high charms work
Done their various roles. My superior magic is working
And these mine enemies are all knit up
And my enemies here are all caught up
In their distractions; they now are in my power;
In their madness; they are now in my power;
And in these fits I leave them, while I visit
And I will leave them in these fits, while I visit
Young Ferdinand, whom they suppose is drown'd,
Young Ferdinand, whom they think is drowned,
And his and mine loved darling.
And my daughter that he and I both love.

Exit above

GONZALO
I' the name of something holy, sir, why stand you
In the name of all things holy, sir, why are you
In this strange stare?
Standing here horror-struck?

ALONSO
O, it is monstrous, monstrous:
Oh, it was monstrous, monstrous:
Methought the billows spoke and told me of it;
It seemed to me that the smoke spoke and told me of it;
The winds did sing it to me, and the thunder,
That the winds sang it to me, and the thunder,
That deep and dreadful organ-pipe, pronounced
Which sounds like a deep and dreadful pipe organ, all spoke
The name of Prosper: it did bass my trespass.
The name of Prospero: it announced my crimes with a resonant voice.
Therefore my son i' the ooze is bedded, and

So my son is sunk in the sea, and
I'll seek him deeper than e'er plummet sounded
I'll look for him deeper than the deepest measured depths
And with him there lie mudded.
And lie with him buried in the mud.

Exit

SEBASTIAN
But one fiend at a time,
If it's only by one demon at a time,
I'll fight their legions o'er.
I'll still fight against their army.

ANTONIO
I'll be thy second.
I'll help you.

Exeunt SEBASTIAN, and ANTONIO

GONZALO
All three of them are desperate: their great guilt,
All three of them are desperate: their massive guilt,
Like poison given to work a great time after,
Like a poison that is given to work slowly over time,
Now 'gins to bite the spirits. I do beseech you
Now comes back to haunt them. I be you,
That are of suppler joints, follow them swiftly
Who are more able-bodied, to follow them quickly
And hinder them from what this ecstasy
And stop them from whatever this insanity
May now provoke them to.
May cause them to do.

ADRIAN
Follow, I pray you.
Follow after me, please.

Exeunt

ACT IV

SCENE I.
Before PROSPERO'S cell.
Enter PROSPERO, FERDINAND, and MIRANDA

PROSPERO
If I have too austerely punish'd you,
I have punished you too severely,
Your compensation makes amends, for I
Your repayment will make it better, for I
Have given you here a third of mine own life,
Have just given you a third of my own life,
Or that for which I live; who once again
Or rather, that which I live for; who once again
I tender to thy hand: all thy vexations
I hand over to you: all your hard labor
Were but my trials of thy love and thou
Was only a trial of your love and you
Hast strangely stood the test here, afore Heaven,
Have passed the test unusually well, and, before the eyes of Heaven,
I ratify this my rich gift. O Ferdinand,
I give you the hand of my daughter. Oh, Ferdinand,
Do not smile at me that I boast her off,
Don't smile at me that I brag about her,
For thou shalt find she will outstrip all praise
For you will find that she will surpass all praise
And make it halt behind her.
And make it stop behind her in awe.

FERDINAND
I do believe it
I believe it,
Against an oracle.
Even if a prophet were to say otherwise.

PROSPERO
Then, as my gift and thine own acquisition
Then, as my gift and your very own treasure
Worthily purchased take my daughter: but

Achieved admirably, take my daugher's hand: but
If thou dost break her virgin-knot before
If you take her virginity before
All sanctimonious ceremonies may
Your wedding ceremony is
With full and holy rite be minister'd,
Completely finished in the eyes of God,
No sweet aspersion shall the heavens let fall
The heavens won't shower you with their blessings
To make this contract grow: but barren hate,
To make your marriage grow healthily: but instead, harsh hate,
Sour-eyed disdain and discord shall bestrew
Evil-eyed scorn and conflict will plant
The union of your bed with weeds so loathly
In your bed of sexual union, loathsome weeds instead of flowers,
That you shall hate it both: therefore take heed,
So that you will both hate it: so pay close attention to
As Hymen's lamps shall light you.
The marriage god give his blessing.

FERDINAND
As I hope
The same as I hope
For quiet days, fair issue and long life,
For peaceful days, beautiful children and long life,
With such love as 'tis now, the murkiest den,
With the love that we have now, I can tell you that not even the darkest pit,
The most opportune place, the strong'st suggestion.
The most opportune moment, the strongest suggestion
Our worser genius can, shall never melt
From the devil on my shoulder, will ever change
Mine honour into lust, to take away
My honor into lust, and take away
The edge of that day's celebration
The passion of our wedding day
When I shall think: or Phoebus' steeds are founder'd,
When I will be thinking in anticipation of that night that the sun god's chariot horses must be lame
Or Night kept chain'd below.
Or that Night has been chained below the horizon.

PROSPERO
Fairly spoke.
That was well spoken.
Sit then and talk with her; she is thine own.

Sit then and talk with her; she is your fiancé now.
What, Ariel! my industrious servant, Ariel!
Hello Ariel! My hard working servant, Ariel!

Enter ARIEL

ARIEL
What would my potent master? here I am.
What is it, my powerful master? Here I am.

PROSPERO
Thou and thy meaner fellows your last service
You and your lower-ranked fellow-spirits performed your last task
Did worthily perform; and I must use you
Very admirably; and I must use you
In such another trick. Go bring the rabble,
In another trick of the same kind. Go get the rest of the gang,
O'er whom I give thee power, here to this place:
Over whom I give you power, and bring them here:
Incite them to quick motion; for I must
Encourage them to move quickly; for I must
Bestow upon the eyes of this young couple
Present for this young couple's viewing
Some vanity of mine art: it is my promise,
Some small display of my magic: I promised to do so,
And they expect it from me.
And they expect it from me.

ARIEL
Presently?
Right now?

PROSPERO
Ay, with a twink.
Yes, in just the wink of an eye.

ARIEL
Before you can say 'come' and 'go,'
Before you can say 'come' and 'go',
And breathe twice and cry 'so, so,'
Breath twice and yell out 'so, so,'
Each one, tripping on his toe,
Every one of us, tripping over our feet,
Will be here with mop and mow.

Will be here pouting and grimacing.
Do you love me, master? no?
You love me master, don't you?

PROSPERO
Dearly my delicate Ariel. Do not approach
I love you dearly, my excellent Ariel. Don't come
Till thou dost hear me call.
Until you hear me call.

ARIEL
Well, I conceive.
Well, I understand.

Exit

PROSPERO
Look thou be true; do not give dalliance
Look you too, be true to one another; don't give flirting
Too much the rein: the strongest oaths are straw
Too much freedom: the strongest oaths easily go up in flames
To the fire i' the blood: be more abstemious,
In the fires of passion: be more self-disciplined,
Or else, good night your vow!
Or else, you can say good bye to your wedding vows!

FERDINAND
I warrant you sir;
I promise you sir;
The white cold virgin snow upon my heart
The white modest virgin snow of your daughter's love in my heart
Abates the ardour of my liver.
Dampens the passion in my loins.

PROSPERO
Well.
Good then.
Now come, my Ariel! bring a corollary,
Now come with me, my Ariel! Bring a companion,
Rather than want a spirit: appear and pertly!
Rather than be without a fellow-spirit: appear and quickly!
No tongue! all eyes! be silent.
Don't speak! Just watch! Be Silent.

Soft music

Enter IRIS

IRIS

Ceres, most bounteous lady, thy rich leas
Cerse, goddess of the harvest, most giving lady, your rich meadows
Of wheat, rye, barley, vetches, oats and pease;
Of wheat, rye, barley, hay, oats and peas;
Thy turfy mountains, where live nibbling sheep,
Your grassy mountains, where sheep live nibbling,
And flat meads thatch'd with stover, them to keep;
And flat meadows covered with winter-straw, to feed your sheep;
Thy banks with pioned and twilled brims,
Your hills with trenched and tangled borders,
Which spongy April at thy hest betrims,
Which rainy April embellishes at your command,
To make cold nymphs chaste crowns; and thy broom -groves,
With flowers to make virgin nymphs' innocent crowns; and your groves of yellow-flowered shrubs,
Whose shadow the dismissed bachelor loves,
Whose shade the rejected young man loves,
Being lass-lorn: thy pole-clipt vineyard;
Having been discarded by his sweetheart: your vineyard with poles covered in vines;
And thy sea-marge, sterile and rocky-hard,
And the coast of the sea, bleak and rocky,
Where thou thyself dost air;--the queen o' the sky,
Where you the goddess yourself enjoy the fresh air;--the godess of the sky,
Whose watery arch and messenger am I,
As I am the sky's messenger and rainbow,
Bids thee leave these, and with her sovereign grace,
Asks you to leave your people, and together with the ruling goddess,
Here on this grass-plot, in this very place,
Come and have fun here on this field, in this very place:
To come and sport: her peacocks fly amain:
Her peacocks fly here at full speed:
Approach, rich Ceres, her to entertain.
Come here, rich Ceres, to welcome her.

Enter CERES

CERES

Hail, many-colour'd messenger, that ne'er
Hello, rainbow colored messenger, that has never
Dost disobey the wife of Jupiter;

Disobeyed the wife of Jove, the god of thunder;
Who with thy saffron wings upon my flowers
You, who with your golden wings
Diffusest honey-drops, refreshing showers,
Spread drops of honey over my flowers, refreshing showers,
And with each end of thy blue bow dost crown
And with each end of your rainbow you put the finishing touch on
My bosky acres and my unshrubb'd down,
My bushy acres and my treeless hills,
Rich scarf to my proud earth; why hath thy queen
You are like a beautiful scarf to my wonderful earth; why has your queen
Summon'd me hither, to this short-grass'd green?
Summoned me here, to this neatly trimmed lawn?

IRIS
A contract of true love to celebrate;
To celebrate a marriage of true love;
And some donation freely to estate
And to present some freely given gifts
On the blest lovers.
To the blessed lovers.

CERES
Tell me, heavenly bow,
Tell me, holy rainbow,
If Venus or her son, as thou dost know,
Do Venus, the goddess of love, or her son, as far as you know,
Do now attend the queen? Since they did plot
Come with the queen? Since they designed
The means that dusky Dis my daughter got,
The plan for the dark god of the underworld to take my daughter,
Her and her blind boy's scandal'd company
I have rejected her and her blind son's
I have forsworn.
Immoral company.

IRIS
Of her society
Don't be afraid
Be not afraid: I met her deity
Of seeing those two: I saw that goddess
Cutting the clouds towards Paphos and her son
Traveling through the clouds toward the city Paphos on Cyprus with her son
Dove-drawn with her. Here thought they to have done

In a dove-drawn chariot. Here they were, thinking they had put
Some wanton charm upon this man and maid,
Some obscene spell on the man and girl,
Whose vows are, that no bed-right shall be paid
Who have promised that there with be no sexual union
Till Hymen's torch be lighted: but vain;
Until the marriage god has given his blessing: but the goddess and her son did so in vain;
Mars's hot minion is returned again;
Venus, the god Mars's mistress, has come back again;
Her waspish-headed son has broke his arrows,
Her spiteful son has broken his love-arrows,
Swears he will shoot no more but play with sparrows
And swears he won't shoot them any more but instead will play with sparrows
And be a boy right out.
And by a normal little boy.

CERES
High'st queen of state,
High queen of the gods,
Great Juno, comes; I know her by her gait.
The great Juno, comes forward; I know the sound of her walk.

Enter JUNO

JUNO
How does my bounteous sister? Go with me
How are you my bountiful sister? Come with me
To bless this twain, that they may prosperous be
To bless these two, so that they may be successful
And honour'd in their issue.
And honored with their family.

They sing:

JUNO
Honour, riches, marriage-blessing,
Honor, riches, marriage-blessing,
Long continuance, and increasing,
Long life, and more,
Hourly joys be still upon you!
Joys every hour for you forever!
Juno sings her blessings upon you.
Juno sings her blessing for you.

CERES

Earth's increase, foison plenty,
Earth's growth, abundance a plenty,
Barns and garners never empty,
With barns and granaries never empty,
Vines and clustering bunches growing,
Vines growing clustering bunches of grapes,
Plants with goodly burthen bowing;
Plants bending with ample fruits;
Spring come to you at the farthest
May spring come to you at the very
In the very end of harvest!
End of the harvest!
Scarcity and want shall shun you;
Shortage and desire will avoid you;
Ceres' blessing so is on you.
Ceres's blessing is also on you.

FERDINAND

This is a most majestic vision, and
This is an incredibly magnificent sight, and
Harmoniously charmingly. May I be bold
Pleasant and enchanting. If I may ask without offending you,
To think these spirits?
Are these spirits?

PROSPERO

Spirits, which by mine art
Spirits, which with my magic
I have from their confines call'd to enact
I have called out of their imprisonment to perform
My present fancies.
My current whims.

FERDINAND

Let me live here ever;
Let me live here forever;
So rare a wonder'd father and a wife
Such a rare father who performs these wonders and a wife
Makes this place Paradise.
Who makes this place a paradise.

Juno and Ceres whisper, and send Iris on employment

PROSPERO

Sweet, now, silence!
Now, my darling be silent!
Juno and Ceres whisper seriously;
Juno and Ceres are whispering seriously;
There's something else to do: hush, and be mute,
There's something else to do: hush, and be silent,
Or else our spell is marr'd.
Or else our spell will be ruined.

IRIS

You nymphs, call'd Naiads, of the windring brooks,
The nymphs of the winding steams, called Naiads,
With your sedged crowns and ever-harmless looks,
With your crowns woven from reeds and always harmless looks,
Leave your crisp channels and on this green land
I ask you to leave your rippling waters and come to this green land
Answer your summons; Juno does command:
To answer your summons; Juno commands you:
Come, temperate nymphs, and help to celebrate
Come here, gentle-natured nymphs, and help to celebrate
A contract of true love; be not too late.
A marriage of true love; don't be too late.

Enter certain Nymphs

You sunburnt sicklemen, of August weary,
Sunburnt, harvesting men, weary from the August harvest,
Come hither from the furrow and be merry:
Come here from the plowed fields and be happy:
Make holiday; your rye-straw hats put on
Celebrate; put on your straw hats
And these fresh nymphs encounter every one
And take a partner from these fresh nymphs
In country footing.
For a country dance.

Enter certain Reapers, properly habited: they join with the Nymphs in a graceful dance; towards the end whereof PROSPERO starts suddenly, and speaks; after which, to a strange, hollow, and confused noise, they heavily vanish

"[Enter some Reapers (harvesters), properly dressed: they join with the Nymphs in a graceful dance; toward the end of which PROSPERO suddenly is startled, and speaks; after which, there is a strange, hollow, and confused noise, and they suddenly vanish.]"

PROSPERO

[Aside] I had forgot that foul conspiracy
[Aside] I forgot about that terrible conspiracy
Of the beast Caliban and his confederates
Of the slave Caliban and his companions
Against my life: the minute of their plot
Against my life: the time for their plan
Is almost come.
Is almost here.

[To the Spirits] Well done! avoid; no more!
[To the Spirits] Well done! Leave; you're done!

FERDINAND

This is strange: your father's in some passion
This is strange: your father is in some sort of fit
That works him strongly.
That is making him act strangely.

MIRANDA

Never till this day
Never until today have
Saw I him touch'd with anger so distemper'd.
I seen him affected with such distressed anger.

PROSPERO

You do look, my son, in a moved sort,
You, my son, look as if some mood has upset you,
As if you were dismay'd: be cheerful, sir.
As if you were dismayed; be cheerful, sir.
Our revels now are ended. These our actors,
Our festivities have now ended. Our actors here,
As I foretold you, were all spirits and
As I told you before, were all spirits and
Are melted into air, into thin air:
Have melted into thin air, right into thin air:
And, like the baseless fabric of this vision,
And, like the unsubstantial material that this vision was made from,
The cloud-capp'd towers, the gorgeous palaces,
The towers in the clouds, the gorgeous palaces,
The solemn temples, the great globe itself,
The sacred temples, and the whole earth itself,
Ye all which it inherit, shall dissolve

Yes, all who live here, will disappear
And, like this insubstantial pageant faded,
And, like this imaginary spectacle, which has faded,
Leave not a rack behind. We are such stuff
Without leaving a single cloud behind. We are made of the same stuff
As dreams are made on, and our little life
That dreams are made of, and our little life
Is rounded with a sleep. Sir, I am vex'd;
Finished in sleep. Sir, I am irritated;
Bear with my weakness; my old brain is troubled:
Tolerate my weakness; my old mind is troubled:
Be not disturb'd with my infirmity:
Don't be disturbed by my frailty:
If you be pleased, retire into my cell
If you would like, go back into my cell
And there repose: a turn or two I'll walk,
And relax there: I'll walk a little bit,
To still my beating mind.
To calm my pounding mind.

FERDINAND & MIRANDA
We wish your peace.
We hope you can find some peace.

Exeunt

PROSPERO
Come with a thought. I thank thee, Ariel: come.
Come here as fast as a thought. Thank you, Ariel: come here.

Enter ARIEL

ARIEL
Thy thoughts I cleave to. What's thy pleasure?
It's your thoughts I obey. What do you wish?

PROSPERO
Spirit,
Spirit,
We must prepare to meet with Caliban.
We must prepare to meet with Caliban.

ARIEL
Ay, my commander: when I presented Ceres,

Yes, my commander: when I acted as Ceres,
I thought to have told thee of it, but I fear'd
I thought about telling you about it, but I was afraid
Lest I might anger thee.
That it might anger you.

PROSPERO
Say again, where didst thou leave these varlets?
Tell me again, where did you last see those rascals?

ARIEL
I told you, sir, they were red-hot with drinking;
I told you, sir, they were red faced with drinking;
So full of valour that they smote the air
So full of heroism that they smacked the air
For breathing in their faces; beat the ground
Because it breathed in their faces; they best the ground
For kissing of their feet; yet always bending
For touching their feet; but always turning
Towards their project. Then I beat my tabour;
Towards their plan. Then I played my drum;
At which, like unback'd colts, they prick'd
At which, like untrained colts, they turned
their ears,
Their ears,
Advanced their eyelids, lifted up their noses
Raised their eyelids, and lifted up their noses
As they smelt music: so I charm'd their ears
As if they could smell the music: so I cast a spell on their ears
That calf-like they my lowing follow'd through
So that they would follow my music like cows through
Tooth'd briers, sharp furzes, pricking goss and thorns,
Thorny briers, spiny shrubs, prickly weeds and thorns,
Which entered their frail shins: at last I left them
Which stuck in their weak shins: finally I left them
I' the filthy-mantled pool beyond your cell,
In the filth-covered pool on the other side your cell,
There dancing up to the chins, that the foul lake
Dancing in the water up to their chins, so that the dirty lake
O'erstunk their feet.
Stuck worse than their feet.

PROSPERO
This was well done, my bird.

That was done well, my spirit.
Thy shape invisible retain thou still:
Keep yourself invisible still:
The trumpery in my house, go bring it hither,
Go bring the fancy clothes from my house here,
For stale to catch these thieves.
As a decoy to catch these thieves.

ARIEL
I go, I go.
I'm going, I'm going.

Exit

PROSPERO
A devil, a born devil, on whose nature
Caliban, he's a devil, he was born a devil, whose character
Nurture can never stick; on whom my pains,
Teaching can never change; on whom my efforts,
Humanely taken, all, all lost, quite lost;
Compassionately undertake, were all wasted, very wasted;
And as with age his body uglier grows,
And as his body grows uglier with age,
So his mind cankers. I will plague them all,
His mind decays as well. I will torment them all
Even to roaring.
To the point of screaming

Re-enter ARIEL, loaden with glistering apparel, & c

"[Re-enter ARIEL, carrying the glittering clothing, etc.]"

Come, hang them on this line.
Come on, hang those on this lime tree.

PROSPERO and ARIEL remain invisible. Enter CALIBAN, STEPHANO, and TRINCULO, all wet

CALIBAN
Pray you, tread softly, that the blind mole may not
Please, walk quietly, so that not even a blind mole could
Hear a foot fall: we now are near his cell.
Hear a footstep: we are now close to his cell.

STEPHANO

Monster, your fairy, which you say is
Monster, your island fairy-music, which you say is
a harmless fairy, has done little better than
Just a harmless fairy-song, has done nothing better than
played the Jack with us.
Play a practical joke on us.

TRINCULO

Monster, I do smell all horse-piss; at
Monster, I smell completely like horse-piss;
which my nose is in great indignation.
Which my nose is very offended by.

STEPHANO

So is mine. Do you hear, monster? If I should take
So is mine. Do you hear that, monster? If I happen to take
a displeasure against you, look you,--
A disliking to you, look at you,--

TRINCULO

Thou wert but a lost monster.
You would be only a ruined monster.

CALIBAN

Good my lord, give me thy favour still.
My good lord, continue to think well of me.
Be patient, for the prize I'll bring thee to
Be patient, because the prize that I'll bring to you
Shall hoodwink this mischance: therefore speak softly.
Will cover up all this misfortune: so speak quietly.
All's hush'd as midnight yet.
Everything is as silent as midnight here.

TRINCULO

Ay, but to lose our bottles in the pool,--
Yes, but to loose our wine bottles in the pool,--

STEPHANO

There is not only disgrace and dishonour in that,
That was not only a disgrace and a dishonor,
monster, but an infinite loss.
Monster, but also a terrible loss.

TRINCULO

That's more to me than my wetting: yet this is your
That means more to me than getting wet: and that was what you called
harmless fairy, monster.
A harmless fairy-song, monster.

STEPHANO
I will fetch off my bottle, though I be o'er ears
I will get my bottle back, even if I am drowned
for my labour.
For my effort.

CALIBAN
Prithee, my king, be quiet. Seest thou here,
Please, my king, be quiet. See this here,
This is the mouth o' the cell: no noise, and enter.
This is the entrance of the cell: don't make any noise, and go in.
Do that good mischief which may make this island
Do that good kind of crime that will make this island
Thine own for ever, and I, thy Caliban,
Yours forever, and I, your Caliban,
For aye thy foot-licker.
Will forever worship you.

STEPHANO
Give me thy hand. I do begin to have bloody thoughts.
Give me your hand. I am beginning to have blood-thirsty thoughts.

TRINCULO
O king Stephano! O peer! O worthy Stephano! Look
Oh, king Stephano! Oh, nobleman! Oh, admirable Stephano! Look
what a wardrobe here is for thee!
At this wardrobe that is here for you!

CALIBAN
Let it alone, thou fool; it is but trash.
Leave it alone, you fool; it's only trash.

TRINCULO
O, ho, monster! we know what belongs to a frippery.
Oh, really, Monster! We can tell what belongs to a thrift-store.
O king Stephano!
Oh, king Stephano!

STEPHANO

Put off that gown, Trinculo; by this hand, I'll have
Put down that tunic, Trinculo; I swear by this hand, I'll have
that gown.
That tunic.

TRINCULO
Thy grace shall have it.
You will have it, your grace.

CALIBAN
The dropsy drown this fool! What do you mean
May disease kill this fool! Why are you
To dote thus on such luggage? Let's alone
So enamored with this stuff? Let's leave it alone
And do the murder first: if he awake,
And do the murder first: if he awakens,
From toe to crown he'll fill our skins with pinches,
He'll have us pinched from our toes to our heads,
Make us strange stuff.
And turn us into strange fabrics.

STEPHANO
Be you quiet, monster. Mistress line,
Be quite, monster. Mistress lime tree,
is not this my jerkin? Now is the jerkin under
Isn't this my jacket? Oh, and now the jacket underneath
the line: now, jerkin, you are like to lose your
You miss lime tree. Now, jacket, you will probably lose your
hair and prove a bald jerkin.
Hair and turn into a bald jacket for being underneath there!

TRINCULO
Do, do: we steal by line and level, an't like your grace.
Carry on, carry on: we'll it steal with great care, if you so desire, your grace.

STEPHANO
I thank thee for that jest; here's a garment for't:
I thank your for that joke; here's a piece of clothing in exchange;
wit shall not go unrewarded while I am king of this
Humor will not go unrewarded while I am king of this
country. 'Steal by line and level' is an excellent
Country. 'Steal it with great care' is an excellent
pass of pate; there's another garment for't.
Use of your thoughts; here's another piece of clothing for it.

TRINCULO
Monster, come, put some lime upon your fingers, and
Monster, come here, put some sticky stuff on your fingers, and
away with the rest.
Steal the rest.

CALIBAN
I will have none on't: we shall lose our time,
I won't do that: we are losing time,
And all be turn'd to barnacles, or to apes
And will all be turned into barnacles, or into apes
With foreheads villanous low.
With terribly low foreheads.

STEPHANO
Monster, lay-to your fingers: help to bear this
Monster, use your fingers: help us carry this
away where my hogshead of wine is, or I'll turn you
Away to where my barrel of wine is, or I'll exile you
out of my kingdom: go to, carry this.
From my kingdom: get to work, carry this.

TRINCULO
And this.
And this.

STEPHANO
Ay, and this.
Yes, and this.

A noise of hunters heard. Enter divers Spirits, in shape of dogs and hounds, and hunt them about, PROSPERO and ARIEL setting them on

"[The sound of hunters is heard. Enter many different Spirits, in the shape of dogs and hounds, and hunt after them. PRSOPERP and ARIEL encourage them on, calling out the dogs names]"

PROSPERO
Hey, Mountain, hey!
Hey, Mountain, hey!

ARIEL
Silver! There it goes, Silver!
Silver! There it goes, Silver!

PROSPERO
Fury, Fury! there, Tyrant, there! hark! hark!
Fury, Fury! Right there, Tyrant! Listen! Listen!

CALIBAN, STEPHANO, and TRINCULO, are driven out

Go charge my goblins that they grind their joints
Go tell my gablins to torment their joints
With dry convulsions, shorten up their sinews
With severe seizures, tighten up their muscles
With aged cramps, and more pinch-spotted make them
With craps like that from old age, and make them more spotted with bruises from pinching
Than pard or cat o' mountain.
Than a leopard or mountain lion.

ARIEL
Hark, they roar!
Listen, they're screaming!

PROSPERO
Let them be hunted soundly. At this hour
Let them be hunted completely. At this time
Lie at my mercy all mine enemies:
All my enemies are at my mercy:
Shortly shall all my labours end, and thou
Soon all my work will end, and you
Shalt have the air at freedom: for a little
Will have your freedom: for just a little while longer
Follow, and do me service.
Follow me, and do my bidding.

Exeunt

ACT V

SCENE I.
Before PROSPERO'S cell.
Enter PROSPERO in his magic robes, and ARIEL

PROSPERO
Now does my project gather to a head:
Now my plan is coming to a head:
My charms crack not; my spirits obey; and time
My spells are not breaking; my spirits are obeying; and time
Goes upright with his carriage. How's the day?
Carries his burden easily. What time is it?

ARIEL
On the sixth hour; at which time, my lord,
Six o'clock; this is the time, my lord,
You said our work should cease.
That you said our work would end.

PROSPERO
I did say so,
I did say that,
When first I raised the tempest. Say, my spirit,
When I first called up the tempest. Tell me, my spirit,
How fares the king and's followers?
How are the kind and his followers managing?

ARIEL
Confined together
All put up together
In the same fashion as you gave in charge,
In the exact way your ordered,
Just as you left them; all prisoners, sir,
Just as you left them; they are all prisoners, sir,
In the line-grove which weather-fends your cell;
In the grove of time trees that stands around your cell;
They cannot budge till your release. The king,
They cannot move until you release them. The king,
His brother and yours, abide all three distracted

His brother and yrour bother all remain confused
And the remainder mourning over them,
And the rest of the group are worrying over them,
Brimful of sorrow and dismay; but chiefly
Completely overtaken with sorrow and panic; but mostly
Him that you term'd, sir, 'The good old lord Gonzalo;'
The one you called, 'Thee good old lord Gonzalo,' sir;
His tears run down his beard, like winter's drops
His tears are running down into his beard, like winter rain runs
From eaves of reeds. Your charm so strongly works 'em
Off of a thatched roof. Your spell holds them so strongly
That if you now beheld them, your affections
That if you looked at them now, your feelings towards them would change
Would become tender.
and become kinder.

PROSPERO
Dost thou think so, spirit?
Do you think so, spirit?

ARIEL
Mine would, sir, were I human.
My feelings would, sir, if I were human.

PROSPERO
And mine shall.
And so will mine.
Hast thou, which art but air, a touch, a feeling
If you—who are only air—have had a sense, a feeling
Of their afflictions, and shall not myself,
Of their suffering, then how can't I,
One of their kind, that relish all as sharply,
As a fellow man, who have sense that are just as sharp,
Passion as they, be kindlier moved than thou art?
And feels as they do, be more moved than you are?
Though with their high wrongs I am struck to the quick,
Though with their mighty crimes I was hurt to the core,
Yet with my nobler reason 'gaitist my fury
Still since my more dignified good sense can overcome my anger
Do I take part: the rarer action is
I will take action: the more special action is
In virtue than in vengeance: they being penitent,
Being virtuous not revenge: as they are remorseful,
The sole drift of my purpose doth extend

The rest of my plan will not go
Not a frown further. Go release them, Ariel:
Any further. Go release them, Ariel:
My charms I'll break, their senses I'll restore,
I will break my spells, and I'll restore their senses,
And they shall be themselves.
And they will be themselves.

ARIEL
I'll fetch them, sir.
I'll go get them, sir.

Exit

PROSPERO
Ye elves of hills, brooks, standing lakes and groves,
You elves of the hills, the streams, the still lakes and the groves of trees,
And ye that on the sands with printless foot
And you that without a footprint on the sand
Do chase the ebbing Neptune and do fly him
Chase the sea god as he flows away from the shore, and flee from him
When he comes back; you demi-puppets that
When he comes back; you little fairies that
By moonshine do the green sour ringlets make,
In the moonlight make fairy rings in the grass with your dancing,
Whereof the ewe not bites, and you whose pastime
Where the sheep will not eat, and you whose entertainment
Is to make midnight mushrooms, that rejoice
Is to make midnight mushrooms, who celebrate when
To hear the solemn curfew; by whose aid,
You hear the evening bell; who have helped,
Weak masters though ye be, I have bedimm'd
Though you are poor helpers, me to cover with clouds
The noontide sun, call'd forth the mutinous winds,
The sun at noon, call forward the restless winds,
And 'twixt the green sea and the azured vault
And between the green sea and the blue sky
Set roaring war: to the dread rattling thunder
Instigate a frightful war: I gave fire
Have I given fire and rifted Jove's stout oak
To the terrible rattling thunder, and split apart the thunder god's own sturdy oak tree
With his own bolt; the strong-based promontory
With his own thunderbolt; I made the solid mountain top
Have I made shake and by the spurs pluck'd up

Shake and by pick up by the roots
The pine and cedar: graves at my command
The pine and cedar: at my command graves
Have waked their sleepers, oped, and let 'em forth
Have awoken their dead, opened and let them out
By my so potent art. But this rough magic
By my powerful magic. But this harsh magic
I here abjure, and, when I have required
I now swear to abandon, and, after I have commanded
Some heavenly music, which even now I do,
Some heavenly music to play, which I am doing right now,
To work mine end upon their senses that
In order to work on their minds for my purpose that
This airy charm is for, I'll break my staff,
This magical spell is meant for, after this I will break my staff
Bury it certain fathoms in the earth,
And bury it several miles deep in the earth,
And deeper than did ever plummet sound
And deeper than has even been measured
I'll drown my book.
I'll throw my magic book into the sea.

Solemn music

Re-enter ARIEL before: then ALONSO, with a frantic gesture, attended by GONZALO; SEBASTIAN and ANTONIO in like manner, attended by ADRIAN and FRANCISCO they all enter the circle which PROSPERO had made, and there stand charmed; which PROSPERO observing, speaks:

"[Serious music plays.

Re-enter ARIEL first: and afterwards ALONSO gesturing frantically, followed by GONSALO; SEBASTIAN and ANTONIO enter in a similar manner to Alonso, and are followed by ADRIAN and FRANCISCO. They all enter the circle which PROSPERO has made, and stand there under a magic spell; which PROSPERO sees and speaks:]"

A solemn air and the best comforter
Now allow a serious song and the best treatment
To an unsettled fancy cure thy brains,
For a disturbed mind cure your brains,
Now useless, boil'd within thy skull! There stand,
Which are now useless and boiling in your skull! There you stand,
For you are spell-stopp'd.

Because you are spellbound.
Holy Gonzalo, honourable man,
Holy Gonzalo, honorable man,
Mine eyes, even sociable to the show of thine,
My eyes, in sympathy with your tears,
Fall fellowly drops. The charm dissolves apace,
Are crying similar tears. The spell will dissolve quickly,
And as the morning steals upon the night,
And just as the morning takes over the night,
Melting the darkness, so their rising senses
Lighting the darkness, so will their minds awaken
Begin to chase the ignorant fumes that mantle
And begin to chase the ignorant haze that covers over
Their clearer reason. O good Gonzalo,
Their clear judgment. Oh, good Gonzalo,
My true preserver, and a loyal sir
My true savior, and a loyal man
To him you follow'st! I will pay thy graces
To him who you follow! I will show you my respect
Home both in word and deed. Most cruelly
Fully both in words and actions. Very cruelly
Didst thou, Alonso, use me and my daughter:
Did you, Alonso, use me and my daughter:
Thy brother was a furtherer in the act.
Your brother was a supporter of this endeavor.
Thou art pinch'd fort now, Sebastian. Flesh and blood,
You suffer for it now, Sebastian. My own flesh and blood,
You, brother mine, that entertain'd ambition,
You, my brother, you held in mind only ambition
Expell'd remorse and nature; who, with Sebastian,
And sent away remorse and natural brotherly affection; who, along with Sebastian,
Whose inward pinches therefore are most strong,
Suffers inside quite terribly because of this,
Would here have kill'd your king; I do forgive thee,
Would have killed you king here; I forgive you,
Unnatural though thou art. Their understanding
Even though you lack the feelings of brotherhood. These men's understanding
Begins to swell, and the approaching tide
Is beginning to rise up in them, and the coming tide of realization
Will shortly fill the reasonable shore
Will soon fill their inner shores of good sense
That now lies foul and muddy. Not one of them
That now are dreadful and muddy. Not one of them
That yet looks on me, or would know me Ariel,

Who looks at me yet, or would recognize me. Ariel,
Fetch me the hat and rapier in my cell:
Bring me the hat and sword from my cel;:
I will discase me, and myself present
I will shed my disguise, and present myself
As I was sometime Milan: quickly, spirit;
As I once was in Milan: quickly, spirit;
Thou shalt ere long be free.
Before long you will be free.

ARIEL sings and helps to attire him

ARIEL singing
Where the bee sucks. there suck I:
Where the bee drinks, I drink there too:
In a cowslip's bell I lie;
In a bell shaped flower I lie;
There I couch when owls do cry.
There I hide when owls are hooting.
On the bat's back I do fly
On the back of a bat I fly
After summer merrily.
Happily chasing after summer.
Merrily, merrily shall I live now
Happily, happily I will live now
Under the
Under the
blossom that hangs on the bough.
Blossom that hangs on the tree branch.

PROSPERO
Why, that's my dainty Ariel! I shall miss thee:
Well, there's my excellent Ariel! I will miss you:
But yet thou shalt have freedom: so, so, so.
But you will still have your freedom: so, so, so.
To the king's ship, invisible as thou art:
Go to the king's ship, invisible like you are now:
There shalt thou find the mariners asleep
There you will find the sailors asleep
Under the hatches; the master and the boatswain
Under the hatches; the boat-master and the boatswain,
Being awake, enforce them to this place,
When they are awake, bring them to this place,
And presently, I prithee.

And immediately, please.

ARIEL
I drink the air before me, and return
I will drink down the air in front of me, and return
Or ere your pulse twice beat.
Before your pulse even beats twice.

Exit

GONZALO
All torment, trouble, wonder and amazement
Only torment, trouble, wonder and amazement
Inhabits here: some heavenly power guide us
Live here: some heavenly god, guide us
Out of this fearful country!
Out of this terrible country!

PROSPERO
Behold, sir king,
Sir king, look here at
The wronged Duke of Milan, Prospero:
The mistreated Duke of Milan, Prospero:
For more assurance that a living prince
So that your will be assured that a living man
Does now speak to thee, I embrace thy body;
Is speaking to you now, I will embrace you;
And to thee and thy company I bid
And the you and your company I bid
A hearty welcome.
A good welcome.

ALONSO
Whether thou best he or no,
Whether or not you are him,
Or some enchanted trifle to abuse me,
Or some enchanted little spell to fool me,
As late I have been, I not know: thy pulse
As I have been lately, I don't know: your heart
Beats as of flesh and blood; and, since I saw thee,
Beats like you are flesh and blood; and, since I saw you,
The affliction of my mind amends, with which,
The trouble in my mind has gotten better, from what
I fear, a madness held me: this must crave,

I fear was a madness that had come over me: this demands
An if this be at all, a most strange story.
A very strange story, if this is really happening.
Thy dukedom I resign and do entreat
I will leave your dukedom and ask
Thou pardon me my wrongs. But how should Prospero
You to forgive my crimes. But how could Prospero
Be living and be here?
Be alive and be here on this island?

PROSPERO
First, noble friend,
First, noble friend,
Let me embrace thine age, whose honour cannot
Let me embrace your old body, whose honor cannot
Be measured or confined.
Be measured or limited.

GONZALO
Whether this be
Whether this is real
Or be not, I'll not swear.
Or not, I cannot tell.

PROSPERO
You do yet taste
You do still feel
Some subtilties o' the isle, that will not let you
Some of the effects of the island, that will not let you
Believe things certain. Welcome, my friends all!
Believe things for certain. Welcome, all my friends!
[Aside to SEBASTIAN and ANTONIO] But you, my brace of lords, were I so minded,
[Aside to SEBASTIAN and ANTONIO] But you, my pair of lords, If I wanted to
I here could pluck his highness' frown upon you
I could bring down his highness' anger on you now
And justify you traitors: at this time
And prove you to be traitors: right now
I will tell no tales.
I will not tell him of it.

SEBASTIAN
[Aside] The devil speaks in him.
[Aside] The devil speaks through him.

PROSPERO
No.
No.
For you, most wicked sir, whom to call brother
For you, wicked man, who if I called you my brother
Would even infect my mouth, I do forgive
It would make my mouth sick, I forgive you
Thy rankest fault; all of them; and require
Your most serious mistakes; all of them; and demand
My dukedom of thee, which perforce, I know,
My dukedom from you, which without a choice, I know,
Thou must restore.
You must give back to me.

ALONSO
If thou be'st Prospero,
If you are Prospero.
Give us particulars of thy preservation;
Tell us the details of your escape;
How thou hast met us here, who three hours since
How you found us here, who three hours ago
Were wreck'd upon this shore; where I have lost—
Were ship wrecked on this island; where I have lost—
How sharp the point of this remembrance is!—
How painful the memory of it is!—
My dear son Ferdinand.
My dear son Ferdinand.

PROSPERO
I am woe for't, sir.
I am sorry for it, sir.

ALONSO
Irreparable is the loss, and patience
The loss is beyond repair, and even Patience
Says it is past her cure.
Says that she can't cure it.

PROSPERO
I rather think
I think that
You have not sought her help, of whose soft grace
You have not really asked for her help, from whose good will
For the like loss I have her sovereign aid

I have her supreme assistance with my similar loss
And rest myself content.
And I can rest calm.

ALONSO
You the like loss!
You had a similar loss!

PROSPERO
As great to me as late; and, supportable
As great to me as it is recent; and, to make
To make the dear loss, have I means much weaker
The dear loss bearable, I have many less resources
Than you may call to comfort you, for I
Than you can call to comfort you, for I
Have lost my daughter.
Have lost my daughter.

ALONSO
A daughter?
A daugher?
O heavens, that they were living both in Naples,
Oh, heavens, if only they were both living in Naples
The king and queen there! that they were, I wish
As the king and queen! So that they could be, I wish
Myself were mudded in that oozy bed
I was myself drowned in the depths of the sea
Where my son lies. When did you lose your daughter?
Where my son lies. When did you lose your daughter?

PROSPERO
In this last tempest. I perceive these lords
In that last storm. I can see that these lords
At this encounter do so much admire
Are so astonished of this encounter
That they devour their reason and scarce think
That they destroy their common sense and hardly think
Their eyes do offices of truth, their words
That their eyes to see the truth, their words
Are natural breath: but, howsoe'er you have
Are spoken from instinct: but, however you have
Been justled from your senses, know for certain
Been knocked away from your senses, know for certain
That I am Prospero and that very duke

That I am Prospero, and the very same duke
Which was thrust forth of Milan, who most strangely
Who was cast out of Milan, who very strangely
Upon this shore, where you were wreck'd, was landed,
Landed on this shore, where you were wrecked,
To be the lord on't. No more yet of this;
To be the lord of the island. I will tell you no more of this yet;
For 'tis a chronicle of day by day,
Because it is a very long story,
Not a relation for a breakfast nor
Not a tale to be told over breakfast, or
Befitting this first meeting. Welcome, sir;
Fit for this first meeting. Welcome, sir;
This cell's my court: here have I few attendants
This little cell is my palace: here I have a few servants
And subjects none abroad: pray you, look in.
And no subject anywhere else: please, look inside.
My dukedom since you have given me again,
Since you have given me my dukedom back,
I will requite you with as good a thing;
I will reward you with something just as good;
At least bring forth a wonder, to content ye
Or at least show you a miracle to satisfy
As much as me my dukedom.
You as much as my dukedom did me.

Here PROSPERO discovers FERDINAND and MIRANDA playing at chess

MIRANDA
Sweet lord, you play me false.
Sweet husband, you are cheating.

FERDINAND
No, my dear'st love,
No, my dearest love,
I would not for the world.
I wouldn't do that for the world.

MIRANDA
Yes, for a score of kingdoms you should wrangle,
Yes, you could argue for twenty kingdoms
And I would call it, fair play.
And I would defend you, calling it fair play.

ALONSO
If this prove
If this turns out to be
A vision of the Island, one dear son
A vision from the Island, my dear son
Shall I twice lose.
I will lose for a second time.

SEBASTIAN
A most high miracle!
A very mighty miracle!

FERDINAND (seeing ALONSO)
Though the seas threaten, they are merciful;
Though the seas may be menacing, they are also merciful;
I have cursed them without cause.
I have cursed them for taking my father without cause.

Kneels

ALONSO
Now all the blessings
Now may all the blessings
Of a glad father compass thee about!
Of a happy father surround you!
Arise, and say how thou camest here.
Stand up, and tell me how you came to be here.

MIRANDA
O, wonder!
Oh, miracle!
How many goodly creatures are there here!
How many good men are here!
How beauteous mankind is! O brave new world,
How beautiful mankind is! Oh, what a brave new world,
That has such people in't!
That has such people in it!

PROSPERO
'Tis new to thee.
It is only new to you.

ALONSO
What is this maid with whom thou wast at play?

Who is this lady that you were playing chess with?
Your eld'st acquaintance cannot be three hours:
You cannot have known anyone here for more than three hours:
Is she the goddess that hath sever'd us,
Is she the goddess that tore us apart
And brought us thus together?
And brought us together again?

FERDINAND
Sir, she is mortal;
Sir, she is human;
But by immortal Providence she's mine:
But by God, she is now my wife:
I chose her when I could not ask my father
I chose her when I could not ask my father
For his advice, nor thought I had one. She
For his advice, nor did I even think that I had a father anymore. She
Is daughter to this famous Duke of Milan,
Is the daughter of this famous Duke of Milan,
Of whom so often I have heard renown,
Who I have heard talked of so often,
But never saw before; of whom I have
But had never seen before; from whom I have
Received a second life; and second father
Received a second chance at life; and a second father
This lady makes him to me.
By marriage with his daughter.

ALONSO
I am hers:
And I am her second father:
But, O, how oddly will it sound that I
But, oh, how strange it will sound for me
Must ask my child forgiveness!
To ask my child for forgiveness@

PROSPERO
There, sir, stop:
It's fine, sir, no need:
Let us not burthen our remembrance with
We don't need to burden our memories with
A heaviness that's gone.
A sorrow that's passed.

GONZALO

I have inly wept,
I have wept inwardly,
Or should have spoke ere this. Look down, you god,
Or I would have spoken up earlier. God, look down
And on this couple drop a blessed crown!
And grant this couple a holy crown!
For it is you that have chalk'd forth the way
For you are the one who has marked out the path
Which brought us hither.
That brought us here.

ALONSO

I say, Amen, Gonzalo!
Well said, Gonzalo, Amen!

GONZALO

Was Milan thrust from Milan, that his issue
Was the Duke of Milan cast out of Milan, so that his offspring
Should become kings of Naples? O, rejoice
Would become kings of Naples? Oh, celebrate
Beyond a common joy, and set it down
More than just a common joy, and bring it down
With gold on lasting pillars: In one voyage
In gold as a lasting monument: In one trip
Did Claribel her husband find at Tunis,
Has Claribel found her husband in Tunis,
And Ferdinand, her brother, found a wife
And her brother Ferdinand found a wife
Where he himself was lost, Prospero his dukedom
Where he was himself lost, and Prospero found his dukedom
In a poor isle and all of us ourselves
In this small island, and all of us found ourselves
When no man was his own.
When no man had control of himself.

ALONSO

[To FERDINAND and MIRANDA] Give me your hands:
[To FERDINAND and MIRANDA] Give me your hands:
Let grief and sorrow still embrace his heart
Let grief and sorrow always stay in the heart
That doth not wish you joy!
Of the person who doesn't wish you joy!

GONZALO
Be it so! Amen!
Let it be so! Amen!

Re-enter ARIEL, with the Master and Boatswain amazedly following

O, look, sir, look, sir! here is more of us:
Oh, look, sir, look, sir! There are more of us:
I prophesied, if a gallows were on land,
As I foretold, if there were gallows on land,
This fellow could not drown. Now, blasphemy,
Then this man couldn't drown. Now, blasphemer,
That swear'st grace o'erboard, not an oath on shore?
Who cursed so much that God was cast overboard; do you not have any swear words now on the shore?
Hast thou no mouth by land? What is the news?
Have you no words on land? What's the news?

Boatswain
The best news is, that we have safely found
The best news is that we have safely found
Our king and company; the next, our ship—
The king and his companions; the next news, our ship—
Which, but three glasses since, we gave out split—
Which, only three hours ago, we believed was split in two—
Is tight and yare and bravely rigg'd as when
Is watertight and ready for sea, and as excellently equipped as when
We first put out to sea.
We first went out to sea.

ARIEL
[Aside to PROSPERO] Sir, all this service
[Aside to PROSPERO] Sir, all this repair
Have I done since I went.
I have done since I went to get them.

PROSPERO
[Aside to ARIEL] My tricksy spirit!
[Aside to ARIEL] My clever spirit!

ALONSO
These are not natural events; they strengthen
These are not natural events; they keep going
From strange to stranger. Say, how came you hither?

From strange to even stranger. Tell me, how did you come here?

Boatswain
If I did think, sir, I were well awake,
If I thought, sir, that I was completely awake,
I'ld strive to tell you. We were dead of sleep,
I would try to tell you. We were dead asleep,
And--how we know not--all clapp'd under hatches;
And—we don't know how—all stowed away under the deck;
Where but even now with strange and several noises
Where just now by strange and various noises
Of roaring, shrieking, howling, jingling chains,
Of roaring, shrieking, howling, jingling chains,
And more diversity of sounds, all horrible,
And even more diverse sounds, all horrible,
We were awaked; straightway, at liberty;
We were woken up; immediately free;
Where we, in all her trim, freshly beheld
Where we saw, newly ready to sail,
Our royal, good and gallant ship, our master
Our royal, good and noble ship, with our master
Capering to eye her: on a trice, so please you,
Dancing in front of her: from a moment, if you want to know,
Even in a dream, were we divided from them
Just as in a dream, we were separated from them
And were brought moping hither.
And were brought here bewildered.

ARIEL
[Aside to PROSPERO] Was't well done?
[Aside to PROSPERO] Was it done well?

PROSPERO
[Aside to ARIEL] Bravely, my diligence. Thou shalt be free.
[Aside to ARIEL]Excellently, my diligent service. You will be free.

ALONSO
This is as strange a maze as e'er men trod
This is a maze as strange as any that men have ever walked
And there is in this business more than nature
And in this situation there is more than what nature
Was ever conduct of: some oracle
Could ever control: some intermediary for the gods
Must rectify our knowledge.

Must tell us what is happening.

PROSPERO
Sir, my liege,
Sir, my king,
Do not infest your mind with beating on
Do not trouble your mind with thinking about
The strangeness of this business; at pick'd leisure
The strangeness of his situation; at some specific time,
Which shall be shortly, single I'll resolve you,
Which will be soon, I'll explain everything to you alone,
Which to you shall seem probable, of every
Which will seem possible to you, of every one of
These happen'd accidents; till when, be cheerful
These events which have occurred; until then, be happy
And think of each thing well.
And think well of each event.

[Aside to ARIEL] Come hither, spirit:
[Aside to ARIEL] Come here, spirit;
Set Caliban and his companions free;
Set Caliban and his companions free;
Untie the spell.
Undo the spell.

Exit ARIEL

How fares my gracious sir?
How is my good sir managing?
There are yet missing of your company
There are still missing from your companions
Some few odd lads that you remember not.
A few more servants that you aren't remembering.

Re-enter ARIEL, driving in CALIBAN, STEPHANO and TRINCULO, in their stolen apparel

STEPHANO
Every man shift for all the rest, and
Every man look out for the others, and
let no man take care for himself; for all is
Let no man take care of only himself; because everything is
but fortune. Coragio, bully-monster, coragio!
Lucky. Courage, good monster, courage!

TRINCULO
If these be true spies which I wear in my head,
If the eyes I have in my face are true,
here's a goodly sight.
Then this here is a fine sight.

CALIBAN
O Setebos, these be brave spirits indeed!
Oh, my mother's god Setebos, these are noble spirits indeed!
How fine my master is! I am afraid
How great my new master is! I am afraid
He will chastise me.
He will punish me.

SEBASTIAN
Ha, ha!
Ha, ha!
What things are these, my lord Antonio?
What are these creatures, my lord Antonio?
Will money buy 'em?
Can they be bought with money?

ANTONIO
Very like; one of them
Probably; one of them
Is a plain fish, and, no doubt, marketable.
Is a normal fish, and can be sold, no doubt.

PROSPERO
Mark but the badges of these men, my lords,
But notice the uniforms of these men, my lords,
Then say if they be true. This mis-shapen knave,
Then tell me if they are loyal. This crippled scoundrel,
His mother was a witch, and one so strong
His mother was a witch, and one so strong
That could control the moon, make flows and ebbs,
That she could control the moon, make the tide flow in and out,
And deal in her command without her power.
And share in the moon's power beyond the moon's control.
These three have robb'd me; and this demi-devil—
These three have robbed me; and this half-devil—
For he's a bastard one--had plotted with them
For he's the bastard—has plotted with them
To take my life. Two of these fellows you

To kill me. Two of these men you
Must know and own; this thing of darkness I
Must recognize and acknowledge; this creature of darkness, I
Acknowledge mine.
Acknowledge is mine.

CALIBAN
I shall be pinch'd to death.
I will be tormented to death.

ALONSO
Is not this Stephano, my drunken butler?
Is this not Stephano, my drunken butler?

SEBASTIAN
He is drunk now: where had he wine?
He is drunk even now: where did he get the wine?

ALONSO
And Trinculo is reeling ripe: where should they
And Trinculo is stumbling drunk: where did they
Find this grand liquor that hath gilded 'em?
Find this fine wine that has colored their cheeks?
How camest thou in this pickle?
How did you come to be in this predicament?

TRINCULO
I have been in such a pickle since I
I have been in such a drunken predicament since I
saw you last that I fear me will never out of
Last saw you that I'm afraid it will never leave
my bones: I shall not fear fly-blowing.
My body: I won't even fear that a fly might lay eggs on me.

SEBASTIAN
Why, how now, Stephano!
Well, how's this, Stephano!

STEPHANO
O, touch me not; I am not Stephano, but a cramp.
Oh, don't touch me; I am not Stephano, I am only sore.

PROSPERO
You'ld be king o' the isle, sirrah?

You wanted to be king of this island, man?

STEPHANO
I should have been a sore one then.
I would have been a severe one if I had become king.

ALONSO
This is a strange thing as e'er I look'd on.
He is the strangest man I have ever seen.

Pointing to Caliban

PROSPERO
He is as disproportion'd in his manners
He is as ugly in his character
As in his shape. Go, sirrah, to my cell;
As he is in his shape. Go, man, into my cell;
Take with you your companions; as you look
Take your companions with you; if you are looking
To have my pardon, trim it handsomely.
To receive my forgiveness, clean it up well.

CALIBAN
Ay, that I will; and I'll be wise hereafter
Yes, I will do that; and I'll be wise after this moment on
And seek for grace. What a thrice-double ass
And seek your favor. What a triple-double ass
Was I, to take this drunkard for a god
I was, to mistake this drunkard for a god
And worship this dull fool!
And worship this stupid fool!

PROSPERO
Go to; away!
Get to it; go away!

ALONSO
Hence, and bestow your luggage where you found it.
Go away, and return those goods where you found them.

SEBASTIAN
Or stole it, rather.
Or stole them, rather.

Exeunt CALIBAN, STEPHANO, and TRINCULO

PROSPERO
Sir, I invite your highness and your train
Sir, I invite your highness and your companions
To my poor cell, where you shall take your rest
Into my small cell, where you can stay and rest
For this one night; which, part of it, I'll waste
For just tonight; which in part, I'll spend
With such discourse as, I not doubt, shall make it
With such conversations that it will, I don't doubt, make the night
Go quick away; the story of my life
Go by quickly; the story of my life
And the particular accidents gone by
And the specific events that have passed
Since I came to this isle: and in the morn
Since I came to this island: and in the morning
I'll bring you to your ship and so to Naples,
I'll take you to your ship and you'll be off to Naples,
Where I have hope to see the nuptial
Where I hope to see the wedding
Of these our dear-beloved solemnized;
Of our dear children here made official;
And thence retire me to my Milan, where
And then I will withdraw myself to Milan, where
Every third thought shall be my grave.
A third of my thoughts will be about my death.

ALONSO
I long
I really want
To hear the story of your life, which must
To hear the story of your life, which must
Take the ear strangely.
Sound wonderful to the ear.

PROSPERO
I'll deliver all;
I'll tell you all of it;
And promise you calm seas, auspicious gales
And promise you calm seas and favorable winds
And sail so expeditious that shall catch
And a return sailing so quick that you will catch up to
Your royal fleet far off.

Your royal fleet of ships that are a day from here.
[Aside to ARIEL] My Ariel, chick,
[Aside to ARIEL] My Ariel, child,
That is thy charge: then to the elements
See that they have a good journey, that is your order: then off into the world
Be free, and fare thou well! Please you, draw near.
And be free, and good bye! If you want, come close.

Exeunt

EPILOGUE
SPOKEN BY PROSPERO
Now my charms are all o'erthrown,
Now my spells are all destroyed
And what strength I have's mine own,
And the power that I have is my own,
Which is most faint: now, 'tis true,
Which is very weak: now, it's true,
I must be here confined by you,
That I must be confined to this play by you,
Or sent to Naples. Let me not,
Or sent away to Naples. Don't let me,
Since I have my dukedom got
Since I have now gotten my dukedom back
And pardon'd the deceiver, dwell
And forgiven the man who deceived me, live
In this bare island by your spell;
On this bare island of a stage due to your magic:
But release me from my bands
But release me from my chains
With the help of your good hands:
With the help of your good hands:
Gentle breath of yours my sails
You good words will fill my sails,
Must fill, or else my project fails,
Or else my project has failed,
Which was to please. Now I want
Which was meant to give pleasure. Now I want
Spirits to enforce, art to enchant,
Spirits to command, magic to weild,
And my ending is despair,
And my ending will be in despair,
Unless I be relieved by prayer,

Unless I am saved by prayer,
Which pierces so that it assaults
Which penetrates so far that it convinces
Mercy itself and frees all faults.
Mercy itself and forgives all flaws.
As you from crimes would pardon'd be,
As you would be forgiven of your crimes,
Let your indulgence set me free.
Let your forgiveness set me free.